PLAYING AROUND

As Liz Archer and Eric Neilson had agreed, the next time was slower, each of them exploring the other's body carefully with mouth and hands, with as many senses as they could bring into play, building each other up to a shattering climax, and then finding it together . . .

And the next time she was astride him, riding him hard while he kissed her breasts, bit her nipples and massaged her firm buttocks, gripping them so hard at times that she could swear she would have black-and-blue marks on her butt by morning . . . and that she wouldn't mind a bit.

ANGEL EYES

ANGEL EYES

#3

WOLF PASS

SPEAKING VOLUMES, LLC
NAPLES, FLORIDA
2017

ANGEL EYES
#3 WOLF PASS

ISBN 978-1-61232-585-9

ANGEL EYES

#3

WOLF PASS

Robert J. Randisi

To Anna and Christopher

Prologue

Old Gray Hair lifted his muzzle and sniffed the air carefully, latching on to the scent he was avidly seeking.

Food.

He trotted down the pine-laden hill, following the smell of his next meal. A huge, shambling beast with a heavy black and gray coat, sparkling eyes, and unusually large ears — one of which was missing a piece. He killed for two reasons.

The first was simple: to eat.

The second was also simple, something that all creatures — animal or man — were concerned with: self-preservation.

He had killed cattle and horses for the first reason and men for the second. He preferred the taste of the animals but was not averse to killing a man. Not if his own life depended on it. He would not , however, make a meal of the human corpse once the kill was made. He would make sure that the human was dead and could no longer threaten him. Then he would go off in search of this preferred meal.

The Nez Percé Indians, not a race of people who were faint of heart, called Old Gray Hair a great god. According to their legends, this same wolf had been walking the earth for many years. They revered and respected him, prayed to him, even feared him.

The white men who populated the nearby logging towns and ranches called him a devil.

They hated him.

They hunted him.

They tried to kill him.

They did all of these things with equal futility.

Old Gray Hair stopped near a ranch which ran both cattle and horses and lifted his muzzle to the air once again, searching for the scent of his arch enemy, man. Finding no trace of the enemy, he stealthily approached a small herd of cattle, picked out a fat cow — and dined!

Chapter One

As Liz Archer rode down the main street of Wolf Pass, Montana Territory, pulling her fur-lined jacket tightly around her, she was acutely aware of the orange bandanna tucked inside her collar. The signature of Angel Eyes. Sometimes she wondered why she didn't just throw it away, or at least carry it in her saddlebag. But she knew the reason why. It had been a gift from Tate Gilmore, a man she had tremendous respect for, and more than a little love. Also, to hide it would mean she was ashamed of it. Tucking it into her collar was simply a way to try and stay out of trouble. But when push came to shove, out came the bandanna that brought her luck.

Liz had never been to Montana Territory before, and she found the cold more than a little disconcerting. Still, she needed a place to rest and think, someplace where her reputation might be unknown.

She hoped this was such a place.

She put her bay mare, Blossom, up in the livery stable and carried her saddlebags and rifle to the Wolf Pass Hotel. The hotel was an impressive structure, three stories high, a product of the booming lumber business that made Wolf Pass a prosperous town.

She walked into the lobby, up to the front desk, put her gear down on the floor with the rifle leaning against the desk, and faced the desk clerk.

"May I help you?" he asked.

He was a well-dressed, prissy dude with slicked-back black hair and he reeked of sickly-sweet perfume. He appeared to be in his late twenties, but he was not to Liz Archer's liking at all. Aside from the obvious reasons, the smile on his face was false, and she hated phonies. Still, Liz was used to being noticed, either for her looks or her reputation, and she found his apparent disinterest curiously refreshing.

"I'd like a room, please."

"Surely," the man said, reversing the large register book so she could sign in. She did so, using the first alias that came to mind, Elizabeth Gilmore.

"Yes Miss . . . Gilmore," the man said, turning the book back to him so that he could read it, "and how long do you expect to be staying with us?"

"I don't rightly know," she said. "Maybe a few days, maybe more."

"I see," the man said, "we'll try to make your stay as comfortable as possible. Would you like a room with a bathtub?"

Liz said she would, as her poke had swelled somewhat thanks to the last couple of jobs she'd taken along the way.

"Very well," he said, taking a key from a slot behind him, "you may have room seventeen, on the second floor. Shall I have someone take your . . . belongings?"

"No, that's all right," she said, accepting the key, "I can handle it. Thank you."

"You're very welcome," the man said. "If you're interested in good meals, I can recommend our hotel dining room for breakfast, lunch, and dinner. The finest food in Wolf Pass." He nodded to his left, indicating a doorway that apparently led to the dining room.

"Thank you," she said. "I'll keep it in mind."

"We also have gambling available in the saloon," he added, inclining his head to his left at another doorway.

"Thanks."

She picked up her gear and made her way to the ornate staircase and up to the second floor. Even the hallways were impressive in this hotel, much wider than any other hotel she'd ever seen.

She found her room, put the key in the door, and opened it. All of the extra money must have gone into the hotel's lobby and hallways, because the room was no bigger than any other she'd slept in. Then again, she was obviously not a high roller, and the hotel probably had much fancier rooms for those who could afford them.

There was a knock on the door, and when she opened it there was a teenage boy with a bucket of water. When he saw her his eyes popped open and he stared, openly admiring the tall, blond woman who was easily the most beautiful thing he had ever seen in all his seventeen years.

"Bathwater," he was finally able to stammer.

"Fine," she said, backing away so he could enter. He lugged the bucket to the tub and poured.

"How many trips does it take to fill the tub?"

He looked at her with pleading eyes. "You want it *filled*?"

"Well, not all the way," she said. He explained that it usually took him half a dozen trips to get a reasonable amount of water into the tub. He could do it in less, he offered eagerly, if he carried a bucket in each hand, but she told him he could take his time.

When he had the tub filled to a reasonable level, he asked if there was anything else that he could do for her. She tipped him generously and thanked him, telling him that if she needed anything she'd call.

"My name is Edgar," he said.

"I'll remember, Edgar," she promised.

When he was gone she undressed with intentions of settling into the hot bath, mindful of the fact that it wouldn't be long before the water cooled. That was okay, though. She wasn't looking for a long hot soak; she just wanted to get clean so she could go downstairs and enjoy a good meal.

She wanted to relax, and hoped that this town was the place to do it.

She settled herself into the hot water and decided to just sit quietly for about five minutes. It was moments like this — when she undressed for a bath and had to remove the little hunk of metal in the shape of an ace of spades that hung around her neck—that she thought of Charles Edward Taker—called "Chance" Taker because he was a gambler — the man she had met and come to love in a town called Kingdom Come, Louisiana.

The night Chance had died — shot to death for cheating at cards — he had given Liz the metal ace of spades, and she had been wearing it ever since, even though she regarded that time in her life as a mistake. She had been innocent and naive, and she admitted now that perhaps she had not been *in* love with Chance Taker, because at the time she had not known what love was.

True, she was not sure even now what real love was — could it have been what she felt for Tate Gilmore, a notorious gunman who was somehow a more honest man than Chance Taker had been? But even so, she did not believe *real* love was what she had felt for Chance. What they'd had had been a new experience for her, one that had distracted her from her real goal in life, to avenge herself on the Nolan family for killing *the* family.

After she had killed the man who killed Chance — outdrawn him in the street — she left Louisiana and returned to her quest for vengeance.

That had been over a year ago, and she had aged considerably more than one year in that time. Her reputation had grown at an alarming rate as well, and she needed time away from it.

Time, she hoped, was what she would have here in Wolf Pass.

The water cooled and she soaped herself quickly, then dried her body while observing herself in the almost full-length mirror. She was lovely, she knew, even beautiful. Her breasts were firm, round, and high, and there was just a hint of roundness to her belly. Her hips flared out and tapered to firm thighs and legs. She turned and saw that her behind was rounded and firm. She had the kind of body that was designed for beautiful dresses and gowns, but the only time she had been able to wear them had been when she was masquerading as a whore in Diablo City,

Texas, in order to get close to the Nolans — and that short time she had in Kingdom Come. Since then it had been jeans, cotton shirts . . . trail clothes.

She was also the kind of woman who attracted men easily, the right kind of men and the wrong kind — and the wrong kind never liked being rejected. More than once that situation had degenerated into gunplay — a fool reason for man to die when there were available women all around.

She dressed in clean jeans and a blue cotton shirt, wrapped the orange bandanna around her neck and tucked it inside her collar, and pulled on her boots. Then she strapped on the .34 Colt Paterson, a gun generally regarded as too small to do real damage . . . unless it was in the hands of Angel Eyes.

That had been proven many times during the past year, and undoubtedly — unfortunately — would probably be proven many more, for Liz Archer's way of life could not be changed.

Many had tried, Tate Gilmore had told her — even he — but in the end she always came back to the gun.

Chapter Two

Upon entering the dining room, she saw that a lot of the money that had been saved on the rooms — her kind of room, anyway — had been spent here as well as in the hallways. She saw fancy oil-burning chandeliers and well-dressed waiters. One of the latter bowed to her and showed her to her table.

"Thank you," she said as he held her chair for her.

Across the room she noticed a man dining with a woman. He reminded her of a Norse god she'd once read about. He was obviously tall — she could see that even though he was seated — broad-shouldered, with dark hair and a beard streaked with gray. It was the hair and beard that made her think of that ancient god. He was wearing a suit that had probably cost him more than she'd ordinarily pay for a horse.

During the few moments she watched, two waiters hurried to the man's table, conferred with him, and hurried away, apparently to bring him something that he wanted.

"Who is that man?" she asked her waiter, unable to contain her curiosity.

"Oh, that's Mr. Neilson, miss," the waiter replied politely.

"Neilson?"

"Eric Neilson," the man said. "He owns the biggest ranch in Montana. He has cattle concerns, deals in lumber, and maintains a suite here at the hotel."

"A suite?"

"Yes, miss. On the third floor. There are four suites up there for honored guests."

In other words, she thought, high rollers.

"Does he gamble?"

"Oh no, miss," the man said, then added, "not at the tables, that is. I gather he's something of a gambler when it comes to business."

"And quite successful, from appearances."

"Oh yes, miss, very successful. May I take your order now?"

She ordered something simple — a steak, medium rare, potatoes, coffee, and rolls — in the hopes that it wouldn't deplete her poke by a great deal. She wondered if she shouldn't find out about another hotel in town, one a little less exclusive.

While waiting for her meal, she found herself looking up from time to time and catching Eric Neilson looking her way. She also saw that his dark-haired companion was noticing their exchange of glances — and didn't look pleased. She continued to stare malevolently at Liz while she and Neilson waited for their meals, a stare Liz continued to ignore — which seemed to upset the woman even more.

Finally, she saw the woman turn to Neilson — who was staring even more intently at Liz at the time — and say something in a sharp tone. Neilson answered the woman calmly, without looking at her, and in reply the woman stood up, said, "I don't have to stand for this!" and stormed out of the dining room. Eric Neilson seemed unaffected by her departure and called one of the waiters over. Probably canceling the woman's dinner, Liz decided.

She watched curiously as the waiter left Neilson's table and walked directly across the floor to her table.

"Excuse me, miss."

"Yes?"

"Mr. Neilson has requested that you do him the honor of joining him for dinner."

"Really?" she asked, surprised. She looked over at the man, who lifted a glass to her. "Uh, I don't think — "

"The gentleman wanted me to tell you that he says 'please.' He has ordered too much food and champagne for one person to accommodate."

She'd never heard the word *accommodate* used in place of *eat* and *drink* before. She looked over at the man again. He was handsome, successful, and he could certainly afford a better meal than she had ordered.

"All right," she said, finally, "tell the gentleman I'd be glad to."

"If you will follow me," the waiter said, "I will escort you to the table."

"What about my order?"

"Don't worry, miss. Will you follow me?"

She followed the waiter to Eric Neilson's table. The man

rose as she approached. She could see that he had noticed her gun, but he seemed unconcerned about it.

"I'm very happy you agreed to join me," he said.

"Thank you for inviting me."

The waiter held the chair for her, and once she was seated Neilson returned to his chair as well.

"After all," he went on, "it is your fault that my companion left."

"My fault?" she asked. "How?"

"Ever since you entered the room, I haven't been able to take my eyes off you."

"Oh? I hope it wasn't a long-standing relationship that I broke up."

"Not at all."

"Good. I'd hate to have that on my conscience."

"I hope you like venison," he said, "and champagne, and chocolate mousse."

"They serve a chocolate moose, here?" she asked, frowning.

As if on cue the waiter appeared with a bucket of ice in which reposed a bottle of champagne. He proceeded to open it and pour a little for Neilson to taste. When he approved the waiter filled Liz's glass first, then Neilson's.

"My name is Eric Neilson."

"Liz,"_she said, and then, after an almost imperceptible pause, added, "Gilmore."

"Miss Gilmore." He raised his glass.

"Liz."

"Eric," he replied, and, the amenities dispensed with, finished, "Here's to new friends."

They continued to talk long past dinner and their first bottle of champagne. The dining room had emptied out, but the waiters still lingered, waiting to do Eric Neilson's bidding.

"This is not exactly prime cattle country, is it?" she asked him at one point.

"The prime cattle country, as you put it, is rapidly becoming overstocked," he explained. "Up here, however, the land is untouched. Ideally, the central plains of the Montana Territory would be better, but I stay here because my lumber concerns are here as well."

"Isn't it rough raising cattle up here?"

"Sure it's rough, and it's risky, and a small cattleman wouldn't be able to do it," he explained. "He wouldn't be able to survive the bitter winters here. I, on the other hand, am not a small cattleman. I have a huge herd and can afford to absorb some losses here and there."

"I'm impressed."

He filled her glass with more champagne and said, "That's a start."

Chapter Three

Eric Neilson's suite was huge — what Liz saw of it, that is. When they entered, sometime after dinner, Neilson did not bother turning up a lamp but simply led her by the hand to the equally huge bed.

The decision to go to his room to make love was an unspoken one. It seemed the natural thing for two people who were obviously attracted to one another to do.

When they were standing alongside the bed, he pulled her gently to him and kissed her. She opened her mouth, allowing his tongue to enter, craning her neck against his extreme height. He was taller than she had guessed, at least six-foot-four.

She broke the kiss and stepped back to unbutton her shirt, and Neilson followed her example. When they were naked to the waist, they came together again in a kiss, a tongue-probing kiss that lasted longer than before. She mashed her large, firm breasts against his chest and rubbed up against him, chafing her nipples against his chest hair until they were taut.

"You're all bone and muscle and gristle," she said, rubbing first her mouth and nose and then her hands over his chest. "There's not an ounce of fat on you."

"Can't afford to get fat," he said, palming her firm breasts.

Although he was not overly muscled, his shoulders were broad as she ran her hands over them, and then he suddenly tapered more than a man his size should have. She wondered if he hadn't been sick recently, hadn't lost a lot of weight.

It was not the time to ask, though . . . .

He bent so that he could cover first one breast and then the other with his mouth, and she sighed as his lips described a trail across her neck and then cradled his head while he buried his face between her breasts, kissing and licking and then sucking her swollen nipples.

From there he went lower, unbuckling her belt, pulling off her boots, and helping her with her pants and underthings. In no time he was on his knees in front of her, running his tongue along the glistening, wet petals of her womanhood.

"Oh, Eric," she moaned, putting her hands on his shoulders and leaning heavily on him. She felt that if he should suddenly move away she would surely fall. It was a combination of the champagne and the erotic sensations that were coursing through her body in response to the probings of his educated tongue.

He stood up and lowered her to the bed, where she lay watching him remove his own boots and pants. Her eyes were used to the dark now and they widened with appreciation when she saw his impressive erection. She reached out for it and found it long and smooth with a swollen, mushroomlike head. It seemed to grow hotter and more urgent in her hand and she tugged him closer so that she could take him in her mouth.

"Jesus . . . Elizabeth," he said as she held him with both hands and laved the head of his penis with her tongue. She licked the smooth, rigid length of him up and down several times until finally she took him inside, suckling him, returning the favor of moments ago. She cupped his sac gently and bobbed her head up and down, allowing him to slide deeper into her mouth and then almost out of her mouth, while never quite letting him pop free.

"Damn," he said then, virtually pulling himself from her mouth and joining her on the bed. "You're so beautiful, so damned beautiful."

She was as eager as he, kissing his neck and letting her hands roam over his body. She was running her hands along his back when she encountered what felt like two puckered, horizontal scars.

"Don't worry," he whispered against her neck, "they don't hurt."

She wondered idly where he had gotten them and if they were the cause of his obvious weight loss, but the thought became lost in sensation as he once again nestled comfortably between her legs and plumbed her sensitive depths with his tongue and lips.

"Yes, oh yes," she said, grabbing his head with both hands as he found her swollen clit and fastened his lips to it, sucking gently first and then more firmly. He would suck and then circle it with his tongue and then suck again, and suddenly she was coming, bouncing her butt off the bed and wrapping her hands in his hair, pulling his face tightly against her gushing cunt.

He hovered over her then and she sought out his rigid penis with both hands. Finding it, she wrapped both hands around it and played with the swollen tip with her thumbs. Neilson reached around so that he could cup her smooth flanks and pull her tightly against him, trapping her hands between them and kissing her deeply.

"Eric," she gasped, sliding her mouth just far enough away from him to be able to speak, "please, I can't wait any longer . . ."

"All right, Elizabeth," he said, kissing the corner of her mouth, "but next time we're going to go slower, a lot slower."

"Yes," she whispered as he slid atop her, "yes, next time . . ."

She caught his penis again and tugged it toward her moist tunnel. He slid past her slick lips easily and penetrated all the way with one swift stroke, causing her to gasp and dig into his back with her nails. He reveled in the warmth and tightness of her and began to explore the wonderfully rounded parts of her body as he continued to thrust into her. She loved the feel of him filling her up with his mass, bringing her hips up to meet his every thrust, gasping as the tip of his penis made contact with her core.

"Yes," she gasped, and then "oh, yes," and then, "that's it, that's it, ooh . . ."

He pounded away at her for what seemed like hours, the only sound in the room their labored breathing and the urgent slap, slap, slap of moist flesh on moist flesh. Finally she began to buck beneath him like an unbroken filly, making a keening sound deep in her throat. Neilson, holding her buttocks tightly, still could not control her, until finally her wild bouncing seemed to suck his orgasm from him, bringing a moan from deep inside him and a cry of pure pleasure from her as he filled her with his seed in what appeared to be a never-ending eruption. . . .

As they had agreed, the next time was slower, each of them exploring the other's body carefully with mouth and hands, with as many senses as they could bring into play, building each other up to a shattering climax, and then finding it together. . . .

. . . and the next time *she* was astride *him*, riding *him* hard while he kissed her breasts, bit her nipples, and massaged her firm buttocks, gripping them so hard at times that she could swear she would have black-and-blue marks on her butt by morning . . .
. . . and that she wouldn't mind a bit.

Chapter Four

Liz left the suite during the night without waking Neilson and went back to her own room. She fell onto her bed, pleasantly exhausted, and slept until daylight came streaming through her window to tease her awake. When she awoke she went downstairs to the front desk to arrange for a bath, this time one she could soak in for a long time.

She thought about Eric Neilson during the bath and stopped when she found herself growing excited. Masturbation was not high on her list of pleasures.

"Is Mr. Neilson in his suite?" she asked the clerk when she came down for breakfast.

"I'm sorry, no, Miss Gilmore," he replied. "He went back to his ranch early this morning."

"I see," she said. "Thank you."

She had breakfast in the dining room and then, after bundling up against the cold, spent an uneventful day looking at Wolf Pass.

The town was flourishing and from what she could see would continue to grow unchecked as long as the lumber lasted. By keeping her ears open, she learned that this part of southwestern Montana Territory was rich in Ponderosa pine, most of it on Eric Neilson's land. He also had the largest herd of cattle in these parts.

Over a solitary lunch at a small café it struck her how little talking they had actually done over dinner — and none thereafter. She knew next to nothing about Eric Neilson except that he was a wealthy man, a charming host — and a wonderful lover.

She went back to her hotel and found no messages waiting for her at the desk. At that point she figured that she had indulged — she and Neilson — in a very pleasnt one-night affair, and she had no regrets.

She did some window shopping for the remainder of the afternoon. She hadn't the money to waste on things she'd probably never use — like dresses. Somehow gingham just didn't go with a gunbelt.

It was still relatively early when Liz decided to return to her room. Either that or find a saloon. As a woman, she did not have the luxury of this alternative. Going to a saloon *could* cause trouble — an overamorous cowboy, drunk or not, or worse, someone recognizing her — so she decided to sit in her room with a book she had picked up during her travels: *The Raven and Other Poems* by Edgar Allan Poe.

By the time she had finished ''The Raven'' she decided that this man Poe was a sad soul indeed, and closed the book rather than go on. She had problems enough without Poe's help.

She had kicked off her boots when there was a knock at

the door. She frowned and decided that guessing would be an exercise in futility. It had to be Neilson. Nobody else in town knew her.

She hoped.

She answered the door and the man standing there smiled and asked, "Miss . . . Gilmore?"

"That's right."

The man had obviously gotten her name from the hotel register.

"Can I help you?"

"I'm here with a message from Mr. Neilson." When she didn't respond he said, "Eric Neilson? He's — "

"I know who he is," she said. For some reason she had taken an instant dislike to this man. He seemed to be everything Eric wasn't: he was short, stout, unattractive, and he wore a perpetual smirk, as if he knew something about her that even she didn't know herself.

"Well then, the message is that he would like you to join him at his ranch for a late dinner."

"Really?"

"Apparently," the man said, "you made an impression on him yesterday."

His smirk twitched and she wondered if he knew just how much of an impression she and Neilson had made on each other. Was Eric Neilson the kind who talked about his one-night conquests?

"What kind of impression?"

The man shrugged and said, "You would have to ask him what he liked, Miss Gilmore. Shall I tell him you'll come?"

"Tell him I won't," she said. "I'm very tired and was just about to turn in."

One night in bed didn't entitle Eric Neilson to summon her at a moment's notice.

"I see," the man said, and his tone said plainly that he did not. "In that case, I was instructed to tell you that it was a matter of business."

"What sort of business?"

"Again, you would have to ask him that," the man replied, "but he did say it would be worth a lot of money to you."

"I don't understand any of this."

He shrugged again, and she was becoming more and more annoyed with his manner. It was as if he had expected her to run right out to the ranch without even putting her boots back on.

"I'm sorry — "

Looking more smug than ever, the man said, "He said that I was to use this as a last resort . . . Miss *Archer*?"

She paused a moment, then said, "Tell Mr. Neilson I'll be along shortly."

Pulling on her boots, she marveled at how her hope of a rest in a nice peaceful town where nobody knew her had vanished over one single night's pleasure. Had he known all along who she was?

She strapped on her gun and then added the orange bandanna, tucked inside her collar.

The "messenger" — who had never given *his* name, making her dislike him even more for knowing hers—had given her directions to Neilson's ranch. It was about a half hour's ride southwest of town.

When she reached the ranch she was impressed by the main house, which seemed to be entirely constructed of lumber. There was a man waiting to take her horse from her, testimony to Neilson's efficiency, she supposed. She ascended the three steps to the door and knocked. Neilson opened it, wearing some kind of red silk lounging jacket, and smiled at her.

"Come in," he said, "Miss Angel Eyes."

Chapter Five

He led her to what was either his office or a den.

"Can I offer you a drink?"

"Why not?"

"Brandy?"

"Fine."

He poured two, handed her one, and said, "I apologize."

"For what?"

"For the way I got you up here."

"Why apologize?" she asked. "It was . . . efficient. I understand you're very efficient at everything you do."

"Actually," he said, "that's right. I am. You of all people should know that."

She let that pass.

She was struck again at how wide his shoulders were set, but how he tapered rather drastically from there. She'd ask him about the scars the first chance she got. It was the least he owed her.

"But I still apologize," Neilson said. "It was wrong to . . . to spring it on you like that. I mean I knew who you were. I'm sure there's a good reason why you registered under a different name."

"I thought so at the time," she said wryly. "Now I'm not so sure. Do you think we could get down to *why* you got me out here?"

"You're a beautiful woman, Elizabeth," Neilson said. "Couldn't that be the reason?"

"It could," she said, "but it's not."

"No, you're quite right. It's not."

"Mr. Neilson — "

"*Mister*?" he asked, raising his eyebrows.

"Mr. Neilson," she said again, "thanks for the drink." She handed him the glass, the contents barely touched, and started for the door.

"All right, *Miss* Archer," he called out, "I'll get to the point."

"Fine." She turned to face him just shy of the door.

He walked up to her, holding the glass out, and after a moment she accepted it.

"I have a problem," he said, then quickly amended the statement. "That is, we here in Wolf Pass have a problem."

"Which is?"

"You can probably tell from the name of the town."

"Wolves?"

"We've always had wolves, Miss Archer — "

"Call me Liz," she said with a sigh.

"I prefer Elizabeth."

"Fine."

"We've always had wolves," he continued, "but this is different. This is one particular wolf."

"One wolf is giving you trouble?" she asked. "Hunt him down, that'll solve the problem quick enough."

"I've tried that." He looked grim now. "I sent men after him, and lost quite a few of them. I've lost cattle too."

"You said you could afford to lose some cattle," she reminded him.

"To the weather, yes," he said, "or to disease — but not this way."

"Are there other ranchers with the same problem?"

"There are other ranchers, but none have spreads the size of mine, so none of them have as big a problem as I do. Still, we've tried working together on this, but Gray Hair is still at large."

"Gray Hair?" she asked, surprised. "You've named the animal?"

"Not I," he said, "Old Gray Hair they call him around here. I'm given to understand that he's been around here longer than I have."

"How long have you been here?"

"Over twenty years."

"That's impossible," she scoffed. "A wolf that old couldn't trouble anyone."

"He's said to be older even than that."

In spite of herself she was becoming interested.

"Are you trying to say that there's something mystical about this wolf?"

"The Nez Percé Indians claim that Old Gray Hair is a god."

This time she didn't scoff. She sipped her brandy and then asked, "What has all of this to do with me?"

"I know that you're the young lady who has somehow built herself up a reputation as a gunfighter called Angel

Eyes," he said, facing her and fixing her with a hard stare. "I want to hire you to hunt this animal down for me and kill it."

"If you know who I am," she said, "you know that I don't hire out my gun. I'm not a hunter."

"Tell that to the Nolans," he said. "You hunted them down pretty efficiently."

"That was different."

"All right," he said, putting his glass down and holding both hands out in front of him, palms facing her. "All right, you had your reasons for doing that, and for doing . . . other things that you have a reputation for. I'll give you a reason to hunt Old Gray Hair for me."

"Like what?"

"Money, and lots of it."

"Not interested." She felt an unreasoning anger welling up inside of her. She put her glass down on a table and made for the door again.

"Elizabeth," he called out. She turned with her hand on the doorknob and he said, "I'd prefer that you do this for me willingly."

She stared at him and said, "That implies that you could force me to do it if you wanted to."

He put his glass down and approached her.

"I can."

She dropped her hand from the doorknob and cocked her head. "How?"

"I know who you are," he repeated. "I don't think anyone else in town does."

"How do you know?"

"Oh, I saw you once, but you didn't see me. It was the briefest of encounters — I was passing through a town you were in — but you stick in a man's mind."

"I'm flattered."

"As I said, I'm the only one in town — maybe in Montana Territory — who knows who you are. The fact that you registered at the hotel under an assumed name tells me that you'd like to keep it that way."

She shrugged, trying to appear unconcerned, and said, "I'll move on."

"I'll spread the word," he said. "I'm part owner of the newspaper. Other papers will pick up the news that the notorious Angel Eyes is in Montana Territory."

"You'd do that?"

"I would. I'm sorry, Elizabeth, but I'm desperate."

"If you do that, somebody could end up dead," she said. "Some kid who wants to try me, or me if somebody turns out to be good enough."

"I'm sorry," he said again, helplessly.

She was incensed that this man would have the gall to bed her one night and blackmail her the next.

"All right," she said. "How much?"

"A thousand dollars."

"Not enough."

"Fifteen hundred."

She shook her head.

"Two thousand, then."

He was only increasing by fives, trying to get her cheap.

"Five thousand," she said.

"Five . . . thousand?"

"Take it or leave it. If you don't agree, then I'll take my chances and leave town."

He rubbed his jaw with his right hand, thought it over, then nodded shortly and said, "Done." He walked to the table where she'd left her glass. "Let's seal the bargain with a drink."

"A drink?"

He turned to look at her, "Unless you have some other method in mind?"

She grinned too. "A drink will do—and half of the money in advance."

"You drive a hard bargain, Elizabeth."

"The pot calling the kettle black," she said, walking to him and accepting the drink. "Who was the repulsive man you sent to the hotel with your charming invitation?"

"Repulsive? That was Henry, my . . . foreman, for want of a better word."

"He's your foreman?"

"He's actually much more than that," Neilson said, but he did not elaborate. He raised his glass to her and said, "Is it a deal then?"

"One other thing."

"What?"

"Those scars on your back. They're recent."

"You're observant," he said. "Yes, they're very recent and I'm just starting to put back the weight I lost while convalescing."

She thought she knew the answer now, but she asked anyway. "Where did you get them?"

"Compliments," he said, clinking glasses with her, "of Old Gray Hair."

Chapter Six

Over dinner Neilson told Liz how he had finally had enough of Gray Hair and had taken his rifle and gone out looking for him.

"Only it seemed like he was the one looking for me," he said, "or waiting for me."

"Waiting?"

"Before I knew it he was on me," Neilson said, staring off at something only he could see. "His . . . claws, I guess, were raking my back, but he never . . . never bit into me, you know? He could have killed me — "

"You must have fought him."

He thought that over for a moment and then said, "Yeah, I guess I must have," as if he wasn't really sure. "I must have . . . gotten away from him. Either that or he allowed me to get away."

"Wait a minute. You're talking about this animal like

it . . . has the ability to think. As if you believe that it is intelligent.''

"I don't know," he said, pensively, "maybe he is."

After dinner they went back to his den.

"If you're going to hunt this animal," he said, handing her a glass of brandy, "you'd better treat him like he can think, like he was as smart as you . . . or smarter."

"When do I get the money?"

"What?"

"The first half of the money. When do I get it?"

He glared at her. "Do you want it now?"

"Yes."

He put his drink down and walked stiffly to a painting on the wall, behind which was a wall safe.

"Don't be so upset," she said. "You dictated the terms of this . . . this relationship."

"That's right." He closed the door to the safe with a slam. "I did." He turned and held out a sheaf of bills to her, which she took. "Are you going to count it?"

"I trust you."

The money was in large denominations. She folded the bills and stuffed them into the pocket of her jeans.

"When will you start earning it?"

"I'll get outfitted tomorrow," she said, "and start out the next day. I'll need someone to get me started in the right direction, though. Tell me the last place he's been seen, or something."

"Uh, yes . . ."

His attitude had changed.

"What is it?"

"Well there's one other thing you should know."

"Like what?"

"Like . . . another detail."

She frowned and asked, "Another condition to this blackmail?"

"I guess you could say that."

"What is it?"

"I sent a telegram last week to a man who hunts wolves for a living. A wolfer."

"And?"

"He'll be here tomorrow."

"Then what do you need me for?"

"Between the two of you — "

"Wait a minute," she interrupted. "You want me to hunt the wolf with him? He's the professional. I'll be in his way."

"I doubt that."

"Well then, he'll be in mine."

"You'll do fine," he said.

"How much are you paying him?"

"You can ask him that," Neilson said, "but I wouldn't bother. One of you might get mad."

That meant that one of them was being paid considerably more than the other.

Which one?

"What's this man's name?"

"Page," Neilson said, "Loren Page. He has a reputation — *as* a hunter."

"I've never heard of him."

"Well," Neilson said, "he doesn't hunt . . . men."

"And I do?" She put her glass down so hard that the contents spilled. "Don't believe everything you hear, Eric. You seem like too smart a man to believe in reputations."

"I am," he said, approaching her and taking her by the shoulders. "Can we start over again?"

He pulled her to him and kissed her, and for a moment

she felt herself responding. When *he* felt that she wasn't any longer, he let her go.

"We can start over," she said, "if you'll forget this bargain, this blackmail."

"Elizabeth," he said, "I must be rid of that wolf."

"I can find my way out." She walked to the door of his den. She opened it and then looked at him again.

"I'm sorry it never occurred to you to simply ask."

Chapter Seven

Loren Page was a wolfer. At 37 years of age, he was probably the finest animal hunter in the country — and his specialty was wolves.

He hunted wolves for two simple reasons. One, it was profitable. Two, he preferred their company to that of people.

He respected wolves. He felt that they were highly intelligent creatures, smarter than horses or dogs. Also, they were more honest than people — who were rarely ever honest.

The telegram from Eric Neilson had intrigued him. The animal Neilson called Old Gray Hair was, according to the rancher, smarter than most men, *older* than most men, and considered by the Indians to be a god. An animal like that was worth seeing.

Of course, the telegram could have been purposely written to make him curious. Still, the promise of five hundred dollars simply to go to Wolf Pass in Montana Territory and listen to Neilson's story made the trip worthwhile, even if the story about the wolf was a phony.

He was in a Wyoming logging town called Ten Pines while Eric Neilson and Liz Archer were having dinner. On occasion, he liked to spend time with some people — more specifically, with women. He was with a young lady named Darlene, who had a sleek, supple body, with small, large-nippled breasts, slim hips, long, thin legs, a flat belly, and enough energy for three women. He preferred more meaty women, but Darlene had been the only one available, and after more than than a month out in the wilds, he couldn't wait.

Page was a tall man, with broad shoulders, muscular arms, a broad, hairy chest — and a faint but definite scent of wolves about him.

"If it wasn't for that," Darlene was telling him as she sat astride him, his thick, rigid pole buried deep inside her, "you'd be almost perfect. Can't you get rid of it?"

"Is it that bad?" he asked, reaching up and popping her big nipples between his fingers.

"Oooh," she said, closing her eyes and grinding down on him, "it's not all *that* bad . . . it's just there."

"If I was a bounty hunter," he told her, "and I hunted and killed men, I'd smell like death. Would you prefer that?"

She opened her eyes and stared down at him, but he pinched her nipples hard and brought her mind back to the business at hand.

Sliding his hands beneath her buttocks, he used his great strength to lift her and turn her over, so that now he was on top, and he began to pound away at her. At one point he felt he might be hurting her, which was the reason he usually preferred more full-bodied women. They didn't have to be handled with care, and when he was in the mood for sex, it wasn't usually *gentle* sex.

As was the case now . . .

"I'll be sore for days," Darlene said as she dressed and prepared to leave Page's hotel room. There was very little jiggle to her, which he missed.

"Sorry if I was rough."

"Don't apologize," she said, putting on her shoes. "If you want me again, just call."

"Sure."

She had been paid in advance, so she made for the door and then stopped before stepping out. "Listen, about what I said . . . "

"What?"

"You know, about the smell . . . It really isn't that bad."

"Sure," he said. "Thanks."

She grinned at him and left, and he rolled over in bed and dug the telegram out of his shirt pocket.

So he smelled like a wolf, he thought, lying back in bed with the telegram in his fist. What else was new? How would you catch a wolf if he was able to smell you miles away. In order to hunt wolves, you had to smell like a wolf — and women like Darlene lost their sense of smell when you paid them enough money.

"Five Hundred dollars," he read, "consultation fee."

Maybe he should start charging everybody a consultation fee.

In the morning Page had breakfast in the hotel dining room and then went to the livery to saddle his horse, a big roan that he'd had for two years and never named. He had named a horse once, when he was a young man, and then he'd been forced to eat the animal to stay alive. Since that time he had refrained from naming any of the horses he owned. They were tools like his rifle and his .45. When he hunted he used a Winchester — unless he was hunting larger game, like bear, then he used a Sharps.

He loaded his gear onto the roan. His wolfskins were rolled and tied to the back of his saddle. He would not don them until it was time to hunt.

He wondered if he should have told the girl what the smell of her perfume had been doing to *his* nostrils?

What he had said to her the night before was true, though. He had been in the company of bounty hunters, gunmen, and some lawmen, and they all had the smell of death on them.

He preferred the smell of wolves.

Liz woke the next morning wondering if she shouldn't just saddle Blossom and ride out. By the time Eric Neilson passed the word that she was in Montana Territory, maybe she could be out of it.

Ultimately, though, she decided to stay. Her curiosity about this animal, this Old Gray Hair, was piqued — and at least the wolf wouldn't be shooting back at her.

Moreover, she was a little curious about this wolfer, Loren Page. Meeting him would be a new experience, because she'd never met a man who hunted animals for a living — the four-legged kind, that is.

While she was dressing, her eyes caught the sheaf of bills that Neilson had given her, sitting on the table next to the bed. She had counted it last night. Twenty-five hundred dollars, more than she'd ever had in her hands at one time before — and that amount coming again, after the wolf was dead.

Why not, she thought, picking up the money. Why not make Neilson pay for what he wanted. He was that kind of man anyway, wasn't he? The kind who thought he could buy whatever he wanted. In this case, he was buying a form of vengeance — for what the wolf had done to his spread, and to him.

Neilson's story about his encounter with the wolf fascinated her. She'd seen wolves before, but never one like this one was supposed to be.

So, a new experience lay ahead and Liz Archer was, after all, still a young woman who had a lot of living to do, a lot of new experiences.

And there didn't seem to be any immediate danger of her having to remove her lucky orange bandanna from inside her collar.

Liz was eating breakfast in the hotel dining room when she saw Neilson's ''foreman'', Henry — was that his first name or last? — enter the room and sweep it with his eyes. He smirked when he saw her, and her dislike for him deepened.

He walked across the room and stopped in front of her table.

''Miss Archer,'' he said. ''Good morning.''

Clad in a dark suit and tie and holding a bowler hat in his hands, he wasn't dressed like any ranch foreman she had ever seen before. She studied him carefully and could find no trace of a gun.

''Can I help you?''

''Mr. Neilson asked me to give this to you.'' He took an envelope out of his inner jacket pocket.

"What is it?"

"A hundred dollars expense money. Mr. Neilson doesn't want you paying expenses out of your own pocket."

"That's very nice of him," she said, putting the envelope down next to her plate. "Tell him I said thank you."

"You can tell him that yourself . . . if you agree, that is," he added hastily.

"Agree? To what?"

"To having lunch with him."

"Where?"

"In his suite. He'll be here later on."

"I don't really have time — "

"He thinks you and your . . . partner . . . should meet."

"Is Page here yet?"

"Not yet, but he should be soon. I've made a reservation here at the hotel for him."

Liz picked up her coffee cup and sipped slowly, making Henry wait.

"All right," she said, putting the cup down, "tell him I'll be there."

"Good. One o'clock, unless you find a message for you at the desk stating otherwise."

"Will you be at this meeting?"

He was turning to leave and stopped short when she spoke.

"Of course not," he said, looking at her. "The wolf is none of my concern. Good day, Miss Archer."

If he was the foreman of the ranch, she wondered, turning her attention to her breakfast again, how could he say that?

Chapter Eight

She used the better part of the morning to purchase her stores, food — nothing perishable, because she didn't know how long she'd be out there — extra ammunition for both her rifle and her .34, an extra-thick blanket for the cold, and a couple of heavy shirts for the same reason.

She returned to the hotel and checked at the desk for messages, but found none. She asked the clerk if a man named Loren Page had checked in.

"Oh, yes." The sweet-smelling clerk raised his eyes to the ceiling. "He certainly has."

"Something wrong with him?"

"Nothing a bath couldn't fix," he replied. "Or maybe that wouldn't even help. My God!"

"Maybe that's what he's doing right now."

"I think not. He didn't ask for any water."

Well, she thought, maybe that made sense. When you

hunt a wolf, do you want to smell fresh and make it easy for the animal to get a fix on you?

Apparently this wolfer knew what he was doing.

"I guess all men can't smell like you, friend," she said, and left the man wondering if that had been a compliment.

Liz knocked on the door of suite 4 and Neilson answered it himself. True to his word, Henry was not around, but the wolfer was.

The desk clerk had exaggerated. The smell was there, but it was faint.

The man rose from his seat as Liz entered. He was tall and solid, though not as tall as Neilson. There was a Winchester by his chair, and he wore no sidearm. As Neilson closed the door behind her, Page removed his hat. His hair was black, as was his mustache, which needed a trim. He looked to be in his late thirties, maybe older.

"Elizabeth, this is Loren Page, the wolfer."

Neilson made it sound like a title. She was "Angel Eyes," and this man was "The Wolfer." What did that make Neilson?

"Page, this is Elizabeth Archer."

Page looked a little awkward standing there with his hat in his hand.

"Neilson tells me they call you Angel Eyes," he said finally, and she glared at Neilson. "I'm sorry," Page continued, "but that doesn't mean anything to me — but then, I don't spend much time in towns or reading newspapers."

"That's all right," she said. "Don't apologize. It doesn't really mean all that much to me either."

"I wasn't apologizing," the man said. "I was just stating a fact."

"Is that a habit of yours?"

"Yes."

"Well, don't stop now."

"All right," he said, dropping his hat on the chair he had just vacated. "I'm against this . . . this partnership, and if I understand Neilson right, so are you."

"What do you propose?"

"That one of us pulls out and lets the other one hunt."

"Excuse me," Neilson said, stepping between them. He didn't like the way they were talking as if he weren't in the room — and he didn't like the looks Page and Liz were giving each other, even if they didn't know they were doing it. "If one of you pulls out, I won't pay the other."

Liz looked at Page and said, "Now what do you propose?"

"I hunt alone," Page told both of them, "and I've always done so."

"If you want my money, you'll hunt with Elizabeth."

Page matched stares with Neilson and then Liz before announcing his decision. "All right," he said, "but if she falls behind, I won't wait up for her — "

"I won't."

" — and I'm not doing it for the money. I'm doing it for a look at this wolf-god of yours, Old Gray Hair."

It was odd, but that was one of Liz's reasons as well.

Page looked at her and asked, "Have you picked up any supplies?"

"Yes."

"We'll have to travel light and eat what the land supplies."

She told him what she had bought, and when she got to coffee, he said, "No coffee. No bacon either. Nothing with a distinct smell, or that old wolf will know we're coming for sure."

"All right," she agreed, "you're the expert. We'll leave those things behind."

For a moment she thought she caught a glimmer of

approval in Page's eyes, but it quickly vanished.

"All right, you'd better pick up a good, heavy blanket and some heavy shirts. It's gonna be cold."

"I've already done that."

"Extra ammunition?"

"Yes."

"What kind of rifle?"

"A Winchester."

He looked down at her hip, at the .34 Colt Paterson that Tate Gilmore had given her, and shook his head. "Too small. You won't bring down a wolf with that."

"This is what I wear," she said. "Maybe I'll slow him down and you'll finish him."

"Well, I guess a man-sized gun would be too big for you to use anyway."

She sensed that he was goading her — maybe testing her — and she let the remark pass.

"Well," Neilson said, "I guess you two are partners. Shall we have a drink on it?"

Page and Liz watched each other, and then Page said, "Just one. I've got things to do if I'm going to be ready by morning."

"But lunch — " Neilson started.

"That's not one of the things I have to do," Page said, accepting the glass of brandy proffered by Neilson.

"Maybe Mr. Page wants to take a bath after his long ride," Liz suggested, accepting a glass of brandy.

"No, I don't," Page said abruptly, "and you don't either. I am not going hunting for a wolf with a sweet-smelling woman along. We'll get you some wolfskins to wear, to deaden your scent."

"Might even deaden my sense of smell."

He finished his brandy in a gulp and said, "You'll get

used to it.'' He picked up his hat and his rifle and said,
''I'll meet you in front of the hotel at first light.''

''If we don't see each other before then.''

He put his hat on, touched the brim, and then left the
room.

Neilson said, ''He seems brutish and educated at the
same time.''

''He knows what he's doing,'' she said, putting her
brandy glass down.

''You're not leaving too, are you, Elizabeth?'' He
sounded more than a little disappointed. ''I've got a
wonderful lunch coming up.''

''I think I'll save my appetite until dinner, Eric,'' she
said, walking to the door. ''That might be my last good
meal for a while, and I want to make sure I enjoy it.''

''But I thought that after lunch you and I might be able
to — ''

''You thought wrong.'' She opened the door and faced
him. ''Did you have to tell him who I was?''

''I, uh, was just hedging my bet,'' he said, and at least
he had the good grace to look sheepish.

''I guess the next time I see you it'll be to collect the rest
of my money.''

''Sure.''

''Did you pay Page half in advance too?''

''No,'' Neilson said, not mentioning the ''consultation
fee'' he'd paid the wolfer just before she'd arrived. ''He
won't take any money until after he's done the job, except
for expenses — and he got the same amount for that as you
did.''

As she was about to walk out the door one of the hotel's
bellboy arrived with a cart laden with food.

''Enjoy your lunch, Eric.''

Chapter Nine

After returning the aromatic bacon and coffee to the general store, Liz spent the time between lunch and dinner in her room, cleaning her guns. She hefted her .34 and felt sure that a bullet from it, carefully placed — like right between the eyes — would down the biggest of wolves. In spite of her confidence, though, she knew that the Winchester would be the weapon to use when and if she came face-to-face with Old Gray Hair.

She took out the little .22 New Line Colt that she kept in her saddlebag. Normally, she carried the gun when she felt the need for a hideaway weapon, one she could get to in a hurry. It probably wouldn't be very useful against a huge wolf, but she cleaned it anyway and decided that she would wear it tucked into her belt, out of sight inside her shirt.

At dinnertime she went downstairs to the dining room

and discovered an odd situation. It seemed as if all but one of the patrons were seated on one side of the room, and the only patron seated on the other side was . . .

Loren Page.

She strode across the room to his table and, seeing her coming, he stood up.

"Well, you haven't spent so much time away from people that you don't have any manners," she commented, smiling.

"Would you care to join me?"

"Thank you, yes."

A waiter came over and held her chair for her and took her order. She had the impression that he was holding his breath until he walked away from the table.

"Something wrong with this side of the room?" she asked Page.

"Yes," he said, pouring her a cup of coffee. "I think it's me. Don't you smell it?"

"Wolf?"

He nodded.

"It's not that bad."

"It is if your home has been terrorized by one, like these people's."

"You're saying it's not you, it's just the smell of a wolf, no matter how faint?"

"Well" — he looked down at his trail-worn clothes — "it might be me to a degree. Then again, some of these folks might just be stuck-up."

She turned in her chair to look at some of the people — men frowning, women holding hankies to their noses — and then said, "That looks like a good bet."

The waiter came with their steaks, and they each ordered

a beer. The waiter brought their beers and then hurried away, turning a little blue in the face.

"Eat hearty," Page said, cutting off a large chunk of his own rare steak, "because from here on it's beef jerky and cold beans. We'll build a fire only out of necessity, but we won't be cooking anything."

"You're the expert," she said, cutting off a slice of her medium-rare beef. Watching the wolfer pack his food away, she figured that he probably didn't get too many good, hot meals, and when he did he simply made the most of it.

"You said that upstairs too," he commented, "and it surprised me."

"Why? Because I'm a woman you think I'm going to argue with you?"

"It's been known to happen."

"I guess it has, but we're going to be out there with a wolf that's supposed to be smarter than us, and some kind of a god to boot. You're the man who's made a profession out of hunting wolves, so I'll be following you."

"Why are you doing this?" Page asked.

"Neilson told you what I'm called."

"So?"

"He's threatened to tell everyone if I don't hunt this wolf for him."

"You ashamed of who you are?"

"I'm Elizabeth Archer," she said, "and I'm not ashamed of that. That other name, the one with the reputation, that's not me, but try and convince some overeager kid with a gun who's looking for a rep of his own of that. I don't need Neilson's help in finding trouble, I find plenty of it on my own."

"I guess I see your point."

"What about you?"

"What about me?"

"Neilson tells me you have something of a reputation too — and I guess you must or he wouldn't have sent for you."

"He didn't send for me," Page said stiffly. "He sent me a telegram offering me a job. I came to find out the particulars."

"And the reputation?"

He shrugged. "I usually bag whatever game I'm after."

"That's commendable."

"Not really," he said, looking at her frankly. "I don't go after an animal if I don't think I can catch him."

"And you think you can catch this one?"

"This one," Page said, his eyes shining, "this one intrigues me. I've heard stories about animals like this. Gods, they're called. They can outthink and outlive a man, they say, but I've never had the opportunity to see one before."

"Don't those cases usually have some sort of explanation? Like . . . maybe it's not the same wolf that people have been seeing down through the years?"

"That may well be, Miss Archer — "

"Liz."

"Neilson calls you Elizabeth."

"I prefer Liz — and it matters little to me what Mr. Neilson does."

"Is there something going on there besides business?" he asked, and she was surprised at his perceptiveness.

"No," she said, "there's nothing going on beyond business." Strictly speaking, her affair with Neilson was over, and she didn't feel she was lying when she answered.

"Well, to answer your question, I understand from

Neilson that the animal has a piece missing from one of his ears — and that he has oversized ears.''

"I've heard that everything about him is oversized," she said, "that he's larger than any normal wolf.''

"That may be," Page said, "but those are the things I want to see for myself.''

He put his elbows on the table and leaned forward, and she saw more animation on his face than she had since meeting him.

"This is the closest I've ever gotten to checking out one of these legends myself, Liz," he went on, "and I don't aim to miss it.''

"That's the way I feel too," she said. "I mean, I've been blackmailed into this hunt and I don't like that one bit, but I'm curious about this animal, this . . . myth. I want to see him.''

"Have you ever hunted . . . an animal . . . before?" he asked. The pause between his words spoke volumes to Liz.

"No," she replied, refraining from asking him if he'd ever hunted a man, "never even shot a deer for food, or a rabbit.''

"How do you like the cold?''

"I don't — but don't worry about me, Loren. Can I call you that?''

He made a face and said, "That's my name.''

Again she refrained from asking a question that popped into her mind — if there was something she could call him besides Loren.

Maybe she'd start calling him by his last name, once they were out on the trail.

"Don't worry about me keeping up, or turning back," she said. "Neither one will happen.''

"No," he said, looking into her eyes, "I don't suppose it will."

"Can I ask you a personal question . . . Loren?"

"Sure," he replied, "but your asking it don't mean that I'll answer it."

"How much is Neilson paying you?"

"Liz . . . I don't ever discuss my fee," he announced flatly.

"Oh."

"Why?" he asked. "How much is he paying you?"

"Well, I think I'll adopt the same policy."

"That's fair," he said, without argument.

They had some dessert — apple pie and more coffee — and then, after the waiter had hastily cleared away the dishes, he said, "As civil — as pleasant — as this dinner has been . . . Liz . . . I want you to know that I'm still against this. It's got nothing to do with you being a woman — "

"I didn't think it did," she said, "but don't worry about being against it, because I am too — and it's got nothing to do with you being a man either."

She thought she saw him suppress a smile before he said, "Then we understand each other."

"Perfectly."

"Well," he said then, "maybe not so perfectly."

She studied his face for a moment. "What do you want to know?"

"Just out of curiosity," he said, "why did you accept my invitation to join me for dinner?"

"Well" — she grinned — "if we're being perfectly honest with one another . . ."

"We are."

She stood up from the table and answered, "I figured I

might just as well get used to the wolf smell now as later.''

Page stood up and hurried out after her, wishing he could think of something clever to say.

Old Gray Hair was hungry.

There was a half-moon, and its light reflected off the silver-gray hairs in the old lobo's shaggy hide. Beneath the hair great muscles flexed and he moved forward easily, as if he were gliding rather than running.

He heard the horses even before he smelled them, lifting his moist muzzle and checking the air.

There they were.

He followed his acute senses and, topping a grassy knoll, looked down at the small herd of horses, who, sensing his presence, began to whinny and move about nervously.

Old Gray Hair's tongue flashed out and licked his muzzle, long strings of spittle dripping to the ground. He picked out a big brood mare who was carrying and, muscles bunching, streaked forward at incredible speed.

The herd dispersed in terror and the two men riding night herd did their best to try and contain them. The mare, however, ran off from the main body of the herd, her screams of terror lost amid the others.

Old Gray Hair followed her, loping easily, deliberately waiting until he and his prey were a respectable distance from the others. She couldn't run very fast, not with her burden, so he ran her down easily enough — and dined!

Chapter Ten

"Are you turning in?" Liz asked Page when they reached the lobby.

"I think I'll find a saloon and have a couple of beers first," he replied, shifting his rifle from one hand to the other. She could see now that he still wasn't wearing a sidearm.

"Would you mind if I joined you? I could use a beer."

"I'll even buy," he said, and they walked to the other end of the lobby and entered the saloon.

The saloon was as impressive as the dining room, with gaming tables of all kinds — roulette, faro, blackjack, poker — but they bypassed those and made for the bar.

Liz could feel the eyes upon her, but there was less likelihood of trouble now than there might have been had she entered alone.

Of course, trouble comes in all different forms.

It was Page who became the object of attention after a while. They were halfway through their beers when two men standing at the bar suddenly seemed to take offense at the wolf odor that Page exuded.

"You know, Kyle," one man, shorter and burlier than Page, said aloud, "it ain't bad enough we got that crazy lobo roaming around out there, killing our stock and our friends, but I don't see why we got to put up with the smell right here in town, do you?"

Kyle laughed and said, "You got that right, Billy." Kyle was almost as tall as Loren Page, but he was much slimmer. Both men wore holstered guns that appeared to be in need of care.

"You mind that?" Page asked Liz.

"Me? Why should I mind? They're talking about you."

For a moment she thought that Page was going to let the remarks go by, but suddenly his eyebrows shot up and he said, "They are?"

"Loren — "

Before Page could reply to the remarks, however, the two cowboys started in on Liz.

"Hey, pretty lady," the one named Billy called out. There were several men between Billy and Liz, but now they seemed to melt away from the bar as they smelled trouble.

"Lady," Kyle shouted, 'can't you hear my friend calling you?"

"Why don't you come over here and cuddle up with us, missy," Billy said, leaning on the bar with his elbows. "You think you might need some help getting away from that smell?"

Liz looked down the bar at the two men and said very

deliberately, "No thanks. I like the smell down here much better than what's coming from you."

"Bitch!" Billy snapped, standing up erect.

"Billy — " Kyle said, stepping in front of his friend, but the burlier man pushed him aside impatiently.

"Liz — " Page said, ready to step in front of her.

"It's all right." She put her hand on his chest. "We can just leave."

"I haven't finished my beer," he said.

"Well, I'm leaving," she said. "I don't want any trouble."

She pushed away from the bar and turned to leave, which didn't please Billy.

"Hey, bitch," he called again, "where you going? You're wearing a gun like a man, ain't ya? Where you get off telling me and my friend we smell bad?"

"Take a whiff sometime, friend," Liz told him. "Your last bath must have been given to you by your mama."

"Damn you — " Billy rushed toward her. Page quickly stepped between Liz and the charging man, and they collided. Billy smacked into the wolfer and staggered back.

"Get out of my way, wolf man!" he growled.

"The lady wants to leave, friend," Page said. "Why don't you let her?"

Liz noticed that Page had left his rifle leaning against the bar and would have to stretch to get it.

"All right, wolf man," Billy said, backing up a step, "first you and then your she-wolf. Make a grab for your rifle."

Liz saw Billy's hand move toward his gun. He was slow, but she knew that Page wouldn't be able to get to his rifle in time. Her own had flashed for her gun, but suddenly

Page was a blur of motion. He took two steps toward the man and clamped his left hand down on the other man's gunhand, trapping his gun in his holster.

"Hey — " Billy said, but he was cut off by a vicious backhanded right from the big wolfer that snapped his head straight back. As he started to fall Page snatched his gun out of his holster and tossed it to the man's startled friend, Kyle, who barely caught it.

"You'd better hold that until our friend cools off," Page said to him, "that is, unless you want to use it."

Kyle's eyes moved from Loren Page to Liz Archer, whose gun was in her hand, and shook his head.

"Not me, friend."

Page stepped toward the bar, lifted his beer mug and drained it in one massive gulp, picked up his rifle, and then turned to Liz.

"Come on," he said, "I'll walk you back to your room.'

"Sure," she said, holstering her gun, and they left the saloon together, the center of all attention.

"Sorry you didn't get to finish your drink," Page said when they got upstairs. "It's the last one you'll have for a while. We won't have anything with us on the hunt except water."

"That suits me," she replied, fitting her key into the lock. "I like water just fine."

She pushed the door open a crack, then turned to look at him again.

"You move fast," she said.

"When I have to. You're pretty fast with that gun yourself."

"You saw?"

He nodded. "I didn't figure you wanted to kill that cowboy, so I took his gun away."

They regarded each other silently for a few moments before Liz broke the silence.

"Can I ask you something else — with the understanding that you don't have to answer," she added before he could say it himself.

"Sure, go ahead."

She leaned against the doorframe and asked, "Does anyone ever call you anything but Loren?"

"Sometimes," he said after a moment. "I've been called Lobo Loren."

"Lobo Loren," she said, trying it on for size.

She pushed the door open and he touched her arm. "Liz," he said before she could go inside, "you have tonight to think this over, you know."

She grinned. "I'll see you in the morning, Lobo."

He shrugged, searched for the words that might make her change her mind, and found none. For a moment, she thought that he was going to ask to come in, but finally he settled for saying, "Good night."

"Good night," she said, and entered her room, closing door behind her.

If he *had* asked to come in, she wondered, would she have let him?

Loren Page entered his room at the extreme end of the hall and set his rifle against the wall next to his bed. He removed his clothes and lay down in his longjohns, painfully aware of his erection. He'd had the damned thing ever since dinner and wondered if at any time during the evening Liz Archer had noticed.

Goddamn, but he had never seen a woman to match her, and he didn't need the distraction while he was out there after that wolf.

As he drifted off to sleep he cursed himself for not having asked her if he could go into her room. She might have said no — he did, after all, smell like a wolf — but if she had said yes, at least the goddamned longjohns wouldn't be so tight now.

Chapter Eleven

At Eric Neilson's ranch, Neilson and his ''foreman'' Henry Buckman were conversing in the office-den.

''Do you think they can pull it off?'' Buckman asked.

''They have to, Henry,'' Neilson said. Buckman noticed that the other man's hands were shaking as he poured himself a brandy. ''I need to be rid of that wolf.''

Only Buckman knew that Neilson had not quite recovered from his meeting with Old Gray Hair. The rancher put up a good front in public, but in private his hands started shaking as he thought about the old wolf and how close it had come to killing him.

''I don't want to have to sell and pull out because of some damned animal!''

''If you'd let me post a bounty — ''

''No!'' Neilson snapped. ''That would bring every fool who ever fired a gun out here. Page is a professional, and Liz — well, she's Angel Eyes, ain't she?''

"If you say so, Eric," Buckman said. He moved forward as Neilson went to pour himself another drink and took the decanter from the other man's hand. "Maybe you'd better get some sleep, Eric."

"Sleep?" Neilson said. "Every time I close my eyes I see that damned wolf."

"You need some rest."

"Get me a woman."

"What?"

"A woman, damn it, from town," Neilson said. "When I'm in bed with a woman it's different. It's like the wolf can't . . . can't get to my mind."

"Eric — "

"Do what I ask you, Henry." Neilson grabbed the man's arm. "Please?"

"All right, Eric," Buckman finally said, "all right. I'll get you a woman."

Buckman left and Neilson knew it would be better than an hour and a half before he returned.

He picked up the decanter and poured himself a drink.

Page woke the next morning feeling slightly frustrated and a little angry. He should have *taken* the goddamned woman last night. Now he had to ride along with her and not only keep his hands off her, but his mind as well.

He hoped she remembered not to take a bath.

When Liz tried to check out of the hotel the next morning, the clerk told her that Mr. Neilson was taking care of her bill and that the room would be held for her until she returned.

Outside she found not only Loren Page but Eric Neilson as well. Neilson was holding the reins of her bay, Blossom, while Page was astride his roan. They were traveling without a pack horse, taking just what supplies and stores they could carry on their own horses. Over dinner, Page had explained that a pack animal would slow them down too much. Someone — probably Page — had already secured her part of the burden to her saddle.

"I wanted to wish you luck," Neilson said as she took Blossom's reins from him. ·

"Thanks a lot," she said. "And thanks for taking care of the room."

"It'll be waiting for you when you get back."

There was something else, though. She could sense it in his manner.

"What's wrong?"

"He hit last night."

"The lobo?" Page asked. He had been quiet up until this point, and now he leaned forward in his saddle, already on the hunt.

"Yes," Neilson said. "Old Gray Hair. He scattered a small section of my herd, ran down a mare, and killed her. She was in foal."

Liz winced when he said that.

"Did you have men there?"

"Yes."

"What did they see?"

"Nothing. They were trying to keep the herd from dispersing too much in the dark. It would have been next to impossible to round them up again before daylight," Neilson said, and who was he trying to justify their actions to? He'd bawled the hell out of them for not getting a shot off.

"Give me directions how to get to that location," Page said.

Neilson did, with both Page and Liz listening intently,

and then Page said, "This is good."

"Good?" Neilson snapped. "How the hell do you figure that? I lost a good brood mare and probably a damned prize foal."

That wasn't true, Liz knew. If she had been such a good mare with a prize foal in her belly, she wouldn't have been out there in the first place, but she couldn't blame Neilson for feeling frustrated.

"We'll be able to track him from a fresh kill," Page said. "This may have cost you a mare, but it gives us a place to start."

Liz mounted up and looked at Loren Page, who had taken on a strange look. It was a look she would see on his face — *in his eyes* — for as long as they were on the hunt.

"I guess we'd better get started," she said.

He was wearing a wolfskin jacket and had another in his hands.

"Here." He tossed it to her. "It might be a little big, but it's the smell that counts."

The gamy odor made her wrinkle her nose, but she couldn't help smiling as she thought of the hoopla she and Page might have caused last night had they worn these in the dining room.

Page looked at Neilson then and said, "Have my money ready when we get back."

"You'll be paid," Neilson said, and then added, "Both of you will be paid, just get that lobo."

"Don't worry, Neilson." Loren Page looked over at Liz. "We'll get him."

Liz was surprised to hear him say *we*. She had the feeling that for some reason she had just been accepted as a partner.

Neilson had spent the larger portion of the night screwing a local whore that Buckman had brought back to the house for him. Waiting for her, he had finished the decanter of brandy. In his semidrunken state he had pounded away at the woman until he was too exhausted to continue — despite the fact that he hadn't ejaculated — and had finally drifted off to sleep — all of two hours' sleep, and he still dreamed about that damned wolf!

Luckily, Buckman had gotten the whore out of his bed and out of the house before he'd jerked awake, wide-eyed and drenched with perspiration. When he remembered that he hadn't been able to achieve a climax, he covered his face with his hands. Wasn't it enough that this unholy creature was robbing him of his sleep; did he have to take his manhood as well? It had been fine with Liz Archer, but not before or since.

"You've got to come back with that damned wolf's hide," he said to himself as he watched Page and Liz Archer ride out of town.

God, he needed a good night's sleep — and he needed Angle Eyes back in his bed.

Chapter Twelve

Following the directions that Neilson had given them, they made their way to the scene of Old Gray Hair's last kill and dismounted.

"Why didn't they move the carcass?" Liz asked as she and Page looked down at the dead mare.

"No reason to," Page said, squatting on his heels and examining the ground around the dead horse.

Liz was examining the horse itself. "Don't predators usually tear off a chunk of their kill and take it somewhere safe to eat?"

"Most do, yeah," Page replied, still studying the ground.

"I don't see any pieces missing —" Liz said, starting to circle the animal's corpse. When she saw the horse's underbelly, however, she stopped short.

Page, who hadn't seen it yet, simply said, "He probably preferred the younger meat and tore out the foal."

"That's what he did, all right." Liz closed her eyes for a moment.

"Are you all right?"

Liz had never been pregnant, but she hoped that the mare was dead before the wolf started tearing out her unborn young.

"Yes, I'm fine."

"We've got some good sign to follow," he said, moving around so that he was standing between her and the carcass. "We'd better get moving."

"All right."

Page took one last walk around the dead mare, and then they mounted up and Liz followed the wolfer as the wolfer followed the tracks of Old Gray Hair.

A lot of their traveling that day was uphill, and by the time dusk came they were pretty tired. They came to a flat plain and Page chose it as a good place to camp. Liz took care of the fire while Page picketed the horses, rubbed them down, and fed them. By the time it was dark they had a fire going — for warmth only.

"That's a nice bay you've got," he said, joining her at the fire.

"Thanks. So tell me what we did today, huh? It was my first day as a big-game hunter."

She was still chilly, despite the fire, and she pulled the wolfskin more closely around her. Somehow, she was getting used to the smell.

"All right. This is your first lesson. An animal who knows enough to leave false trails is the most dangerous kind."

"False trails?"

"We tracked him," Page said, "but he's a slick one, this Gray Hair."

"What do you mean?"

"We followed a few false trails today," Page explained.

"Wasn't there some way of telling that they were false?"

"After a while, sure. Then we double back and try to pick up the real trail."

"Are you saying that the legends about this animal are true?"

"I can't give you an opinion on *that* yet," Page said, "but he is a slick one, I'll give him that much."

"It's eerie," she said, looking out into the darkness, "knowing he's out there somewhere and that he's supposed to be some sort of a myth . . . a devil."

"He's a wolf," Page said, and then abandoned what he had been about to say and snapped, "Don't stare into the fire!"

She started and he said, softer, "If you stare into the flames, it'll destroy your night vision. That wolf could come right out of the darkness and you'd never see him."

"Oh," she said, feeling foolish.

Page went back to what he'd been saying before. "Whatever they call him — god, demon, devil — he's still a wolf."

"And you're a wolfer."

Page shrugged and passed her some hard tack, cold beans, and a cup of water. True to his word they had cooked nothing, because the aroma would announce their presence to Old Gray Hair.

"Does that make you natural enemies?"

"No." He shook his head. "Do you know who natural enemies are?"

"Who?"

"Men — and women. We are our own natural enemies. More men are killed by men than are killed by wolves."

"So . . . what about you and the . . . the wolf? What are the two of you?"

"We're . . . adversaries," Page said, searching for the proper words, "opponents."

"You're hunters," Liz said then, "both of you. Predators."

He stared at her for a moment. "My philosophy is, if you're not the hunter, you're the hunted. You were a hunter not long ago, weren't you?"

"Yes," she admitted, "but I'm not proud of it."

"Maybe not, but you did it. The first time I hunted I wasn't proud of it — and I wasn't proud of the fact that I enjoyed it. Fact of the matter is, though, there isn't much else I can do to make a living."

He looked at her then and asked, "What do you do for a living?"

"My reputation says that I — "

"I don't care what your reputation says." Page cut her off. "I told you, I never heard of you or your reputation."

"I . . . just travel around," she said, "taking odd jobs."

"Like this one?"

"I've never hired my gun out, Loren. I do whatever else I have to do, but I've never hired out my gun."

"Why not?"

She bit off a piece of hard tack and chewed thoughtfully. Why not, indeed? She was sure that men like Clay Allison, Les Nolan, and even Tate Gilmore had hired their guns out once or twice during their lives.

"It's what you do best, isn't it?" Page asked. "Fire a gun?"

"I suppose — "

"Where's the harm then in doing what you do best for a living?" She wasn't sure whether he wanted an answer or not, but before she could give him one he said, "Well, that's what I do for a living — what I do best. I hunt."

He finished his water and stood up to clean the tin plate. She quickly spooned the remainder of her beans into her mouth and added her plate as well.

"Do you want an answer to that question?" she asked.

"Which one?"

"Why I don't hire out my gun."

"No, I don't need an answer, as long as you have one for yourself."

"I don't know, Loren," she said, and he looked at her as she asked, "Is there a way to hire out your gun and not have to end up killing somebody?"

He stared at her for a moment and then said frankly, "I don't know, Liz. I guess maybe I . . . don't know what I'm talking about, huh?"

"No," she said, "there's a lot of truth to what you said. Do you make a good living doing what you do best?"

"I get by," he replied. "I can usually pick and choose my jobs. I say no more than I say yes."

"Then maybe you do know what you're talking about," she said, "but you kill animals. I'm not as good a shot with a rifle as I am with this." She touched the .34 on her hip. "If I'm going to kill for a living with this, it would have to be men — and I've killed enough men to know that I don't like doing it, not even for money."

They regarded each other quietly for a few moments and then he said, "You'd better turn in. I'll take the first watch."

"Wake me in two hours — "

"No," he said, "I'll wake you in four. Four straight

hours of sleep will keep us more alert and fresh than two on and two off.''

"All right. You're the boss.''

"No, I'm not,'' Loren Page said, ''We're partners, remember?''

As Liz bedded down near the fire, Loren Page sat across the fire and alternately watched her and looked out into the darkness. He was convinced that Liz's beauty and nearness would be a distraction during the hunt, but more and more he found himself watching her. During the day, while they were riding, she stayed behind him, but here, with the firelight reflecting off her golden hair, it was almost impossible to keep his eyes off her.

This was the first and last time he would go hunting with a woman, no matter how much he was paid or how intrigued he was by the animal.

Or by the woman.

Liz could feel Page's eyes on her and wondered if he would approach her while they were out here together. She wondered why he hadn't approached her that last night in town. Could it be that he'd spent so much time hunting animals that he didn't know how to act with a woman?

Could it be that if and when she became sufficiently curious about — or attracted to — him, she would have to be the one to approach him?

Well, even if that were the case, it would have to wait until they were back in town. This was neither the time nor the place for them to . . . get better acquainted.

Meanwhile, out in the darkness, Old Gray Hair stood on the crest of a slope, sniffing the air carefully, curiously. The smells coming to him were strange. They were wolf smells, but they weren't.

Old Gray Hair was confused.

Chapter Thirteen

When Loren woke Liz, she sat up and pulled the wolfskin tightly around her.

"Tell me something?" she said as Loren settled down on his bedroll.

"What?"

"Just how effective are these skins at fooling the wolves?"

"Not very," he said, stretching his long, lean frame and laying his rifle down beside him.

She stared at him. "Well, why do you wear them then?"

"I don't know," he replied. "Maybe for the same reason you keep your gun clean."

As he closed his eyes, she said, half to herself, "Well, at least they're warm."

In the morning Page woke before Liz could wake him.

"Bet you could use some coffee, huh?" he asked, teasing her.

"Very funny." She stood up and stamped her feet against the cold. "This is the last time I travel north," she said, moving closer to the fire. "From now on it's New Mexico and Texas."

Page was closing up his bedroll and said, "Come back to Montana Territory in the summer. It's just as hot here as it is in Texas."

"Well, all right," she said grudgingly, as if accepting an invitation, "maybe in the summer."

They loaded up their gear and for the first time Liz noticed the leather carrying case among Page's things.

"What's that?"

"That?" he said, picking up the case. He untied the leather thongs that secured it and pulled out a rifle. "That's the Sharps Big .50."

"Don't tell me, let me guess," she said. "You used to hunt buffalo."

"I've hunted buffalo with this, sure, *and* bear. This is what will put Old Gray Hair down, if I can get him in my sights. It's accurate at better than 200 yards."

He handed it to her and she was surprised at how heavy it was.

"I understand they're stamping the new ones with the name Old Reliable on the barrels, but this one has been 'old reliable' to me for years now."

"It's a single-shot?"

"Yes, but one is usually all you need. I've seen buffalo hunters put down fifty big shaggies with fifty shots."

He took the gun back and slid his Winchester into the case instead. From his saddlebag he took out an old Navy

Colt in a worn holster and strapped it on. He wore it high on his hip.

"If I'm gonna carry the Sharps, I usually wear this, and only because the Sharps is a single-shot weapon. You never know when you'll run into two wolves at one time, and that's when this baby becomes a liability — the only time. Besides, I'd hate to have to try and use this." He tapped the Colt. "I'd probably end up shooting myself in the foot."

She doubted it, but didn't comment. She noticed how his eyes almost sparkled when he talked about the Sharps.

"You love that gun, don't you?"

"I love hunting with it, yes," he said. "I've never missed with it."

"That's quite a record."

"Let's hope I can keep it intact."

They mounted up and Liz noticed that Page rode with the big Sharps across his thighs. He hadn't done that yesterday so he must have known somehow that they wouldn't run into Old Gray Hair.

She asked him about it and he said, "Even if he saw us he'd watch us for a while. He could be watching us now."

"You keep talking about him like you believe what they say about him."

"Even if he's *only* as canny and crafty as any other wolf, Liz," he told her, "that makes him dangerous enough."

After that she took to riding with her Winchester across her thighs.

Chapter Fourteen

About the time Liz and Page started out after Old Gray Hair again a man rode into Wolf Pass on a big gray, sporting a pair of pearl-handled Colts. One of the two men who had taunted Loren Page in the saloon, Kyle Hanks, saw him and nudged his friend, Billy Tyler. "Look."

Billy looked and saw the man riding down main street toward the livery.

"Kind of early for new arrivals," he commented. "He must have ridden all night."

"That wouldn't bother him," Kyle said.

"You know him?"

"I think so."

"Who is he?"

"I think he's Frank Logan."

"Frank Logan!"

"I'm pretty sure," Kyle said. "You saw he was riding a gray and wearing pearl handles."

"That'd be Logan, all right," Billy said. "Who'd want to impersonate him? That could get a man killed."

"I wonder who he's here for?" Kyle said aloud.

"Who knows?"

"There might be a way to find out."

"Sure, ask him."

"What would you do if you rode into town at dawn after riding all night?"

"I'd head straight for the hotel since the saloon isn't open yet."

"And if he's Frank Logan, he'll go to the biggest hotel in town."

When Frank Logan entered the lobby of the Wolf Pass Saloon, he noticed the two men standing by the desk talking to the clerk. Carrying his rifle and war bags, he approached the desk and set them down on the floor.

"Room," he said to the clerk.

"Of course." The clerk looked at him nervously. "J-just sign in, please."

Logan did, using his real name since it was obvious that the clerk — and probably the two cowboys who had been talking to him — already knew. The gunman was willing to bet that they were the two men he had seen as he rode into town.

"Your key," the clerk said, handing it to him.

Logan picked up his gear, started for the stairs, and then turned back.

"Maybe you can help me." He addressed all three men.

"Of course," the clerk said. "We'll try."

"I'm looking for a man."

"Who?" Kyle asked.

"A big man," Logan said, "tall but not as heavy as me." Logan was a big, beefy man whose grace belied his size. "You wouldn't be able to miss him. He's a wolfer. His name's Page, Loren Page."

"Oh yes, he's registered —" the clerk began to say, and then he remembered that the man wasn't registered because Mr. Neilson was paying for his room. "He had a room here."

"Had?" Logan frowned and returned to the desk. "What do you mean? Is he gone?"

"He's gone, all right," Kyle said, laughing and looking at his friend. "Gone hunting."

"For what?"

"A wolf," Kyle answered, "what else would he be hunting for?" He felt clever until he saw the look in Logan's eyes.

"You smart off at me, boy, and I'll make you wish your mother was here so's you could hide behind her skirts — and then I'd knock her down to get to you."

"Uh, sure — whadaya want to know?"

"I heard Page was headed this way, but I didn't know why. You got a bad one in this area?"

"The worst," Kyle said. "They call him Old Gray Hair and he's a devil."

"And he's out after him?"

"Yeah, he left yesterday — him and the bitch."

"What bitch?"

"I don't know, some woman who came to town a few days ago. Neilson would know."

"Who's Neilson?"

"Eric Neilson," Kyle said, wishing his friend Billy or the clerk would answer a question once in a while. His mouth was getting dry. "He owns the biggest spread here-abouts, and he's got the biggest grudge against that big lobo."

"How do I find Neilson?"

Kyle gave Logan directions to the Neilson spread, and then the big bounty hunter turned and headed for the stairs.

"Is there a bounty on this wolfer?" Kyle asked, with more curiosity than brains.

"If there was," Logan said from the steps, "you would-n't be able to collect it."

"I don't want it," Kyle said, "but I don't think any more of that smelly wolfer than you do."

Logan turned to face Kyle squarely, still standing on the stairs.

"You got that wrong, friend," he said evenly. "I think about Loren Page, I think about him all the time."

"Yeah, but I mean you don't think *much* of him, do you?"

"You talking about respect?"

"Yeah, that's it," Kyle said, wondering what would happen if he made a break for the door. "You don't respect him?"

"I respect him a hell of a lot," Logan said, starting up the stairs again, "which is why I won't go out after him. I'll just wait for him to come back — and then kill him."

Frank Logan entered his hotel room and did not give it a second glance. It didn't matter to him what kind of shape it was in as long as it had a bed. He'd ridden through the night to get here, hoping to gain some time on Page, the one man he hated most in the world. Now that he was here he was delighted to know that Page had a job hereabouts. Now he could afford to sleep for a while and then just sit

back and wait for Page to come riding back into town —
right into his waiting . . . guns.

He unbuckled his belt and hung the twin pearl-handled
revolvers on the bedpost, where he could reach them easily. Lying down on the bed without even bothering to
remove his boots, he started to drift off to sleep with one
last thought.

He hoped that the wolfer hadn't finally met a wolf that
would be his match.

Chapter Fifteen

Along about evening Page and Liz came within sight of a small log cabin. It was a welcome sight for Liz, because they were now at a higher altitude than they had been the night before when they camped, and the air had an extra bite to it.

They had followed sign all day — *Page* had followed the wolf's sign, *she* had followed Page — and he had led them into an area that was even denser with trees and foliage — more than she had ever seen. The trees seem to slice right into the sky and she couldn't imagine how anyone could cut them down — how anyone could *bear* to, or how they were physically *able* to.

When she mentioned this thought to Page, he said, ''I think what they do sometimes is climb them and start at the top.''

''Climb them?'' she asked, staring at him. ''How do they climb them?''

He shrugged. "I'm a wolfer not a logger."

"It's so dense here . . ."

"Gives him more places to hide," Page told her, and at once she started to dread pitching camp that night.

Now they encountered this cabin.

"What's that doing here?" she asked.

"Who knows," Page said, "but there's one sure way to find out. Come on."

They rode up to the cabin and dismounted, grounding their horses' reins.

"Hello!" Page shouted, knocking on the door. "Anyone here?"

"It doesn't look like it, does it?" Liz said from behind him.

Page tried the door, found it unlocked and pushed it open. They entered and found signs that the cabin had not been inhabited for some time. There was not much furniture except for an overturned table and some chairs, and everything was covered with dust.

"We'll camp here," he said — unnecessarily, since Liz had already decided that *she* was camping inside even if *he* wasn't.

"This is a godsend," Liz said, already feeling the difference in temperature. The windows were intact, and though it was not warm inside, it was better than outside.

"All right," he said, turning to her, "let's get the horses in here with us."

"The horses?" she asked. "In here?"

"Well, I'm sure as hell not going to leave them outside where Old Gray Hair can get at them."

"No, of course not."

"Besides, if you can stay in here with me, you can stay with the horses. They can't smell much worse than I do."

"Than *we* do," she corrected him, and they went out to bring the animals inside.

Once they had a fire going — in the center of the floor and not in the hearth — Page surprised her by telling her she could make coffee.

"Coffee? How come?"

"We're inside," he said, "and using the hearth. We can take a chance that the aroma won't escape."

"What about some bacon?"

He grinned. "Let's not press our luck — but you can take the chill out of some beans."

To Liz it sounded like a veritable feast.

He watched her make the coffee and warm the beans, and he swore again never to hunt with a woman. If he'd been alone, he wouldn't have taken the chance of making the coffee, but he knew that she needed it, even though she hadn't once complained. Oh, he'd teased her about the cold and she'd acknowledged it, but she never once actually complained.

He admired her for that — and found himself desiring her even more, without bothering to try and deny it.

"Thanks," he said as she passed him a hot cup of coffee and a tin plate of warm beans.

"I wonder who lived here last?" she said.

"Loggers, maybe. Are we still on Neilson's land?"

"I don't know. I don't know how much he has."

"Plenty," Page said. "Maybe it was used as a line shack at one time."

"Well, I don't care what it was used for. For the first time in two days I can almost feel my toes."

He put down his empty cup and plate. "Take off your boots."

"What?"

"Take them — here, I'll help you."

He crossed over to her and took hold of one of her feet, taking it between his legs with his back to her. She planted the other on his behind and pushed. They repeated the process and both of her boots were off. That done he sat next to her, took her feet in his lap, and began to rub them.

"Ooh, that feels good." She closed her eyes and set her cup and plate down on the floor. The warmth of his hands and the heat of the fire were making her drowsy.

He kept rubbing her feet and suddenly she felt one of his hands slide up her pants, onto her bare leg. His fingers were cool, but she didn't complain. She kept her eyes closed, waiting to see how far he wanted to go.

She already knew how far *she* wanted to go.

Under normal circumstances she would not have expected a man to want to make love to her, not the way she looked and the way she *smelled* at that moment, but this was something else. They *both* smelled of wolfskins and sweat, and she was not the least bit put off by it.

In fact, during the two days they had been hunting together, she had found herself gradually becoming interested in, attracted to, and then finally excited by the big wolfer. He was a very competent, understanding man, and he was not at all unattractive.

And now he was growing bolder, his entire hand up her right pants leg, caressing her calf. Slowly, he eased his hand out and then took off her socks so that her bare feet were in his hands.

"Liz — " he said then, and even with that one short word his voice sounded husky with desire.

"I know," she said, opening her eyes and looking at him. "I know, Loren."

She went to him then, getting up on her knees, and their mouths met eagerly.

His hands went to her shirt, unbuttoned it, and slid inside to cup her firm breasts. Even the calluses on his hands excited her, and she moaned into his mouth and slid her own hands inside his shirt.

"We shouldn't — " she murmured against his mouth.

"I know."

"The wolf — "

"I know," he said, running his lips over her cheeks and down to her neck. "The door's locked, the windows are closed and — oh damn, I want you, Liz."

"I know," she said. "I want you too."

Page left her long enough to collect both of their bedrolls and laid them down together on the hard-packed dirt floor. She removed her shirt, then moved onto the bedroll with him — both on their knees — and removed his, also peeling his longjohns down to his waist.

He pulled her to him roughly, banging her breasts into his chest and kissing her hard.

"Mmm, easy — " she said, pushing against his chest with her hands.

"I'm sorry," he said quickly. "I'm not used to being gentle — "

"I'll teach you." She kissed him softly on the mouth, "I'll teach you . . ."

She took his face in her hands, gently ran her tongue over his lips, and then kissed him, just an easy touching of the lips at first, but then she opened her mouth and he responded so that she could send her tongue into his mouth, where it fluttered about lightly and, finding his, drew it back into her own mouth.

She told him to lie down on his back and removed his

boots, his pants, and then his longjohns, peeling him naked. She stood up then and let him watch as she took off the remainder of her clothes.

He watched, fascinated, as the light from the fire made her hair and body glow. Her breasts were large and round, firm and more beautiful than anything he'd ever seen. Her nipples were pink and rigid and seemed to be staring at him. Her belly was slightly rounded and the hair between her legs seemed to be on fire. She stepped over him with one foot, then knelt with one knee on either side of his head and said, "Lick me, Loren."

He did, easily at first, enjoying the taste of her, but before he could go further she slid down over his chest until her breasts were dangling full in his face.

"Lick them," she said, putting one of her nipples by his mouth.

He licked first one, then the other, and then she said, "Suck them, bite them — gently — ah, that's it. Hold them with your hands, Loren — oh, who said you couldn't be gentle?"

She pressed her breasts against his chest then, her hard nipples against his coarse hair, and kissed him, more firmly this time. He encircled her with his arms and seemed to make an effort not to squeeze her too tightly.

She slid her hand down over his belly, through the tangle of black pubic hair to his rigid cock, huge and pulsing anxiously, and she took hold of him, sliding her hand up and down, playing with the bulbous head with her thumb, bringing him so near climax that he lifted his hips, expected to explode . . . but she didn't let him.

She moved around so she could lie atop him then and kissed his face, his neck, his chest, enjoying the sweaty he-wolf smell of him. Her lips worked their way down over his belly until she was licking the length of him, holding him at the base with one hand and fondling his balls with the other. He was bigger than Eric Neilson, but not too big for her. She had been taught how to do this by a pimp in Diablo City when she had worked for him as a whore.

How to please a man was the only good thing she had come away from that town with. . . .

He reached down to grasp the back of her head, groaning as she ran her hands along his hairy thighs, digging in with her nails. She continued to work on his turgid shaft with her mouth and rubbed her breasts over his thighs because she enjoyed the way his hair — and he had it all over his body — scraped her sensitive nubs.

"Come up here where I can reach you," he said huskily, sliding his hands underneath her arms and lifting her up over him.

He was strong and he held her just above him so he could lick and suck her nipples, slide his tongue along the valley between them. Her pelvis was tight against his and she could feel his cock, huge and seemingly alive, throbbing, poking at her, trying to find a way to get in. She settled her hands down on either side of him, taking her weight off of him. She lifted her hips so he could slide between her legs and then lowered herself onto him.

"Ahhh, shit . . ." he said, moaning as he glided into her. He couldn't believe how hot she was, and how large he felt. He'd never had such an erection before.

Immediately his hands moved around to cup her buttocks, and she proceeded to ride him easily, just letting him slide all the way in and then almost all the way out, teasing herself as well as him. Her eyes were closed, her breath came in great shuddering waves, and her thighs and legs felt weak. She couldn't remember the last time she had been this excited with a man and she didn't understand why it was so with this one, this wolfer who was almost as much animal as the wolves he hunted. . . .

Or maybe that was it! Maybe there was something about his . . . his restrained ferocity that excited her. Perhaps it was like being locked in a room with a . . . a wolf!

It was as if she were outside herself now, eyes closed, floating, riding him, and suddenly with a great animal groan he took hold of her and they rolled over so that he was on top.

"Gently," she reminded him with her mouth right up against his ear. She could feel that he was as excited as she was, but he was too strong to let him lose control. "Gently . . . I'll tell you when . . ."

He began to move inside of her gently, which was hard for a man who was used to pounding away at a woman. He knew, though, that this woman was different from the other women that he'd ever been with.

This one was different . . . .

Old Gray Hair approached the cabin cautiously, sniffing the air with care. His mouth hung open, spittle dripping to the ground, his hot breath escaping in huge, cloudlike gusts. He moved closer to the cabin, sniffing at its base, at the bottom of the door. He smelled human things, not the least of which was a bitch in heat — but he knew that this was not one of his own kind.

It was his enemy and the wolf chose that moment to strike. . . .

Chapter Sixteen

Page continued to move inside her, easily, slowly, taking her in long, slow strokes until finally she said, "All right, all right, faster."

He increased his speed and she dug her nails into the floor and lifted her hips to him, matching his tempo as it continued to build.

"Jesus, Loren . . ." she moaned. "Harder . . . do it harder . . . now . . ."

He slid his hand beneath her to cup her firm buttocks and, holding her tightly, began to thrust into her while pulling her toward him, using a steady rhythm that fanned the already-kindled flame that was burning deep inside both of them.

He was not by any means inexperienced, she realized, just not used to caring for someone else's pleasure as well as his own. Now she could see that with an iron will he was holding on as long as he could. She ran her palms over the muscles of his back, and when her fingers reached his coccyx and she slid one between his buttocks, he suddenly exploded within her. Scant seconds later she felt her orgasm rushing up from deep inside, and their moans and cries mingled to form a symphony of mutual satisfaction.

"That was incredible," she said, kissing his neck and shoulders.

"You're beautiful," he said with his lips in her hair.

He started to withdraw from her, but she held him tightly and commanded, "Stay inside of me." She put her lips to his ear and then ran her tongue around it.

"No," he said, drawing himself up so he could look down at her. His eyes held a tenderness she had seen when he talked about wolves, and guns. When he spoke it was with something akin to . . . reverence.

"I want you . . ." he said.

"How?"

"Let me show you."

He began running his tongue over her breasts, nibbling her nipples and licking the smooth flesh, but abandoned them quickly enough to explore her body further. No, she thought, running her hands over the back of his neck and his shoulders, closing her eyes against the sensations he was building up inside of her, he is certainly not inexperienced.

He worked his way down over her belly to her loins, where he proceeded to plumb her depths, savoring her heady scent and intoxicating taste. This time he drank deeply of her and then with his tongue he made swift little circles around her straining clit until she was coming again, whimpering and lifting her butt off the bedroll as he continued to probe and lick. . . .

After that they kissed and caressed each other until suddenly he was hard inside of her again, and this time they were like two animals, each seeking their own pleasure with no regard for the other. The only sound in the room was their heavy breathing and the slap-slap-slap of moist flesh on moist flesh as they drove themselves on and on . . . and on.

In the midst of two shattering climaxes, a window suddenly shattered and a long gray-black shape hurtled into the room in a shower of broken glass. . . .

Chapter Seventeen

The shaggy gray animal landed just as Liz and Page broke apart, and he landed *between them*.

Liz felt panic and watched as the animal suddenly veered, banging into Loren and driving him back into the fire. She heard the wolfer cry out as the flames burned his flesh, and then thought about her gun.

The sharp wolf scent immediately made the horses go crazy. They started trying to find a way out of the cabin, adding to the confusion.

The wolf was confused now too. He couldn't seem to make up his mind whether he wanted to go after the humans or the horses.

Liz, feeling the rush of cold air from the broken window chill her body, groped about trying to remember where she had put her .34 or her Winchester.

Page was rolling on the floor, trying to get away from

the fire, but it seemed to follow him. A burning chunk of wood came into contact with the wooden table and it immediately started to burn. Another piece of firewood had rolled against a wall and the flames were climbing toward the ceiling now.

It seemed to take only seconds for the cabin to catch fire, and now smoke was filling the interior.

The horses were scrambling about wildly and the wolf took a swipe at Page's roan, ripping its chest and causing it to scream in pain and horror.

Liz saw her .34 then, hanging on the back of a chair, but as she reached for it Page's roan ran into her, knocking her flat. Dizzy, she looked up and found herself face-to-face with Old Gray Hair.

The wolf's eyes seemed to burn into hers, and they stayed that way for a few moments, oblivious to the fire and the chaos around them.

Suddenly, the wolf bolted toward the window. Liz located her gun, leaped for it, and threw two shots after the animal as it disappeared through the window.

The wolf was gone, but that had no calming effect on the horses, or the situation. Three sides of the cabin were burning now, as was the roof, and Liz knew that they had to get dressed and get out before they were trapped.

"Loren!" she called.

"Here," his voice came from behind her.

She turned and saw that he was in the process of pulling on his pants.

"We've got to get out of here," he shouted to her. "Get dressed!"

It seemed foolish to dress before fleeing the fire, but she knew that they would freeze if they ran from the cabin naked. Quickly she dressed and then looked toward Loren again.

"Get the horses out," he called. "I'll collect all of our gear."

"All right."

She went to the horses, talking to them, reaching for their bridles. Blossom was easy, because she knew that the hands holding her were her mistress's. The roan was more difficult — he was still panicky, and in pain from the wounds on his chest — but he soon responded to Blossom's confidence. Liz took hold of them both and, opening the cabin, let them outside.

Outside she was cautious lest the wolf be there waiting. She wouldn't have put it past the brutish animal.

Satisfied that he was not waiting, she looked back at the cabin, now a sheet of flames. Her saddle came flying through the door, followed by Loren's, and she wished that he'd forget their gear and get *himself* out before it was too late.

After what seemed like years he came running out, carrying their rifles and saddlebags. She secured the horses to a small tree and ran over to him.

"Loren, are you all right?"

"Yes, you?"

"I think so."

His face was black with soot and she knew that he must have burns somewhere.

"Did you see him?"

"Yes."

"Wasn't he magnificent?"

She stared at him now, not at all sure that she had heard him correctly.

"What did you say?"

"He slammed into me and he was so solid, so huge!" he went on, staring at the fire. "Look what he did."

"He knocked you into the fire."

"Yeah," he said, looking at her. "My back . . ."

"Is it painful?"

"Hell yes."

"Let me look — "

"Not now." He brushed her hand away. He hunched his shoulders inside his jacket and skins — probably against the pain — and said, "How are the horses?"

"Frightened, and yours is bleeding."

"Let's have a look."

They went to the horses and Page examined the tears in his roan's chest.

"Could have been worse," he said, grabbing his canteen from his saddle and pouring it out. Water was no problem, since they had passed more than one stream along the way.

Using his hands, he mixed the water with the dirt and then scooped up handfuls and laid them over the horse's injuries.

"That should stop the bleeding when it dries, at least until we can get back to town."

"We're going back?"

"Oh yeah," he said. "Whatever food we had left is in there, and I need another mount — then I'm coming back out."

It sounded to her as if he intended to come back out alone, but she didn't question him now. There would be time for that after his injuries had been seen to.

"We'd better start back now." He looked up at the sky.

"It's dark."

"There's plenty of moonlight, and now that the wolf has had his small victory he may get bolder."

"I fired at him."

"Did you hit him?"

"I don't know."

He walked back to the burning house and found the window the wolf had come through. He studied the ground and said, "There's blood."

"How much?"

"Not much." He squatted on his heels and winced at the pain from his burns. "Could be he was cut by the glass, or could be you popped him one with the .34. If you did . . ." He shook his head and let the rest trail off.

"If I did . . . what?"

"If you did," he said, looking up at her, "all you did was make him mad."

"What do you mean?"

"You saw the size of that brute," he said, standing up. "He's the biggest wolf I've ever seen by far, and if you hit him with that .34, it didn't do much damage, except to change his attitude."

"I still don't — "

"Up to now," he said patiently, "every move he's made has been simply to survive. If he's got a bullet in him, then he's mad . . . and if he's mad, he's ten times as dangerous as he was before."

She stared at him.

"Scary, huh?" he said.

"Hell, yes."

Not far from the cabin Old Gray Hair stopped, lay down, and began licking his left haunch, tasting his own blood and not liking it. Something was hurting him, and he tried using his teeth to get it out, unsuccessfully. He shifted then, so that he was lying with the wounded side against the earth, and he stayed quiet for a long time. Eventually, the bleeding stopped, although the pain persisted.

He knew who had caused him the pain, and now he pictured those beings in his mind, so that he would never forget them.

They had caused him pain, and they would have to pay.

Chapter Eighteen

They fairly staggered into town the next morning, and as they reached the livery the roan suddenly stumbled. Page threw himself free as the animal fell, and then watched as the roan's sides heaved . . . and he died.

"Guess I shouldn't have ridden it," he said, standing over the fallen animal.

"If you hadn't," Liz pointed out, "that might be one of us lying there instead of him."

"Yeah," he said. "Well, I've got to get my rig off him and see about another horse."

"You have to get to the doctor," she said.

"I'll meet you there. Why don't you get cleaned up? After the doctor we'll have something to eat and . . . talk."

"Yes. I think we're going to have to do that."

He looked at her and they both understood that there was going to be one hell of an argument. As she left she heard him telling the liveryman to show him the best he had, because Eric Neilson was footing the bill.

She went back to the hotel and indulged in a quick bath, then put on fresh clothes and went downstairs to find the doctor. As she passed through the lobby she saw Eric Neilson's foreman, Henry — and he saw her.

"Miss Archer," the man said, tipping his bowler. "You're back — you *and* Mr. Page?"

"Yes, but only briefly," she replied. "We'll have to restock and start out again."

"But what happened?" he asked, stepping between her and the door. "Did you see the wolf?"

"Not now, Mr. . . ."

"Buckman," the man said, smiling his oily smile.

"Mr. Buckman," she acknowledged, then went on, "not now. I've got to get over to the . . . doctor's office," she said, wishing immediately that she hadn't.

"The doctor? Are you ill?"

"Mr. Buckman — "

"Mr Neilson will be very interested — "

"Then I'll explain to him when I see him," she snapped. "Now excuse me."

"Surely." He stepped aside with exaggerated politeness.

She brushed past him and went outside before she realized that she did not know where the doctor's office was. Rather than go back in she asked the first person she saw, then followed his directions.

The doctor's name was Miller, and he was working on Page when she entered.

"Miss, you'll have to wait — "

"It's all right," Page said, "she can stay."

This was the first chance she had to see Page's injuries, which were to his back. They looked ugly, red, and blistered, and the doctor was cleaning out the blisters and applying some salve. Over that he put some bandages so that Page could put his shirt back on.

"Afraid you won't be able to take a bath for a while," the doctor said, wrinkling his nose at the same time.

"That's okay, doc," Page said, standing up and sliding his shirt on stiffly. "What do I owe you?"

When the doctor told him, Page referred him to Eric Neilson.

To Liz he said, "Come on, let's get something to eat."

"You're hungry?"

"Starving."

She realized then that she was ravenous as well.

They decided on the small café where Liz had lunched her first day in town, then she told Page that Henry Buckman was at the hotel, and possibly Neilson too.

"I'm not ready to talk to them yet," Page said, and she agreed.

When they were settled at a table with a pot of strong, black coffee and their order in, Liz said, "All right, let's have it."

"I almost got us killed last night."

"You?" she asked. "How can you take the blame for what happened?"

"Because I should have known better," he said. "I let you . . . distract me."

"Well, in case you hadn't noticed, Mr. Page," she replied archly, "I was pretty damn distracted myself."

"I noticed. . . ."

When their food came, they called a momentary truce. After what they'd eaten for the past two days, the hot food deserved all their attention.

"All right," she said when they were almost finished, "let's have the rest of it."

"The rest of what?"

"The rest of the argument. How you want me to stay behind while you go after Old Gray Hair alone. How it'll be safer for the both of us if we're not out there distracting each other. How — "

"If you're worried about the money — "

"I thought you didn't talk about money."

"My money," he corrected her. "I'm talking about your money now."

"Well, I don't talk about money either, remember?"

"Well, I'm the boss, remember? Isn't that what you've been saying all along?"

"Sure, but you convinced me."

"Of what?"

She smiled sweetly and said, "We're partners, remember?"

He frowned at her, then signed. "Shall we go back to the hotel and talk to Mr. Neilson?"

"Why not? I could use some of his brandy right along now."

Chapter Nineteen

Frank Logan couldn't believe his eyes.

He was staring out the window of his room — which overlooked the main street — and he saw Loren Page coming toward the hotel with a beautiful woman who was wearing a gun.

His first instinct was to go downstairs and kill the wolfer, but he remembered his meeting the evening before with Eric Neilson in the rancher's suite. . . .

He had asked the clerk where he could find a man named Neilson, and the man had told him that Mr. Neilson had suite 4, and was in.

Logan knocked on the door, and when a man opened it he said, ''Are you Neilson?''

''No, I am Henry Buckman. Who are you?''

''Logan,'' he said, brushing past the small man.

There was a taller man standing in the center of the room, holding a drink, and he said, "Are you Neilson?"

"I am."

Logan turned to the other man and said, "Get out."

"I don't think — " Buckman began, but Neilson nodded to him and he withdrew, closing the door behind him.

"What can I do for you, Mr. Logan?"

"It's what I can do for you, Neilson."

"What's that?"

"First, how about a drink?"

"Of course." Neilson poured a brandy and handed it to Logan.

"Expensive," Logan said after he sipped it, and Neilson was frankly surprised that the man could tell.

"What is the nature of your business, Mr. Logan?"

"Me? I'm a little like Loren Page, Mr. Neilson. I hunt . . . only I hunt people."

"What has that got to do with me?"

"Well, you see, right now I'm hunting Page, and I understand he's working for you, hunting a wolf."

"That's right."

"Well, I figure it might be worth your while to pay me not to kill him until he bags your wolf."

Neilson stared at him for a few moments and then asked, "Are you serious?"

"I'm real serious. See, I'm gonna kill him one way or the other. It would be to your benefit for me to wait until after he kills your wolf, wouldn't it?"

Ever the practical businessman, Neilson had to agree.

"And I know Page's fees are high," Logan said. "So all you'd have to do is pay me half what you're supposed to pay him . . . and I could always be persuaded to kill him *after* he kills the wolf, and *before* he collects from you.''

Neilson studied Logan for a few moments, and Logan thought he knew what the man was thinking. He was trying to decide if Logan could do what he said he would do, and the rancher finally decided that he could.

''Why do you want to kill Loren Page?'' Neilson asked.

''That's none of your business,'' Logan said, pointing with the hand that was holding the now empty glass.

''Mr. Logan,'' Neilson said, ''would you like another drink?''

Now Logan watched as Page and the woman crossed the street to the hotel, and he could feel his hatred burning hotly inside him.

Still, Page was worth a lot of money to him. All he had to do was wait. He had to check with Neilson and find out if Page was back because he'd killed the wolf or simply to restock on supplies.

He moved away from the window and walked, naked, back to the bed, where the whore was waiting. She was a big woman, with huge, pendulous breasts, big hips, heavy, meaty thighs, and a belly the way he liked it, soft and not flat. He liked to be able to ''feel'' the woman underneath him, and that just wasn't the case with some of those spindly whores.

This one's name was Lola — she said — and as he approached the bed she reached out to stroke his curiously small, though erect penis.

''I never saw such a small one on a man as big as you,'' she said.

''So?''

Logan was not self-conscious about the size of his penis. He did not use it to measure his manhood, and besides, he had never failed to satisfy a woman.

She shrugged and her breasts rippled.

"Nothing, really. I just . . . never did."

She leaned forward and opened her mouth, taking his entire penis in one small gulp, and he reached down to squeeze her breasts while she sucked him.

Eric Neilson was pacing the floor of his suite, and had been doing so ever since Henry Buckman had told him that Liz Archer and Loren Page were back in town.

Had they killed the wolf?

Buckman told Neilson that he didn't think so, that the Archer woman was very evasive and talked about going to the doctor.

"That could only mean one thing," he told Buckman. "They went up against Old Gray Hair and came away second best. She wasn't hurt, you say?"

"It didn't appear so."

"Then it must be Page," Neilson said, and then laughed ironically. "The expert."

Buckman waited patiently for Neilson to decide what to do.

"All right, Henry," the rancher finally said, "go downstairs and wait for them in the lobby, and when they get here bring them straight to me. They've got some explaining to do."

"All right."

After Buckman left, Neilson poured himself another drink and wondered about Liz and Page. He wanted Liz Archer, he decided, almost as much as he wanted that wolf dead. It had taken a woman like her to make him feel like a man again — something that hadn't happened since his encounter with the wolf. He'd seen the way she and the wolfer had looked at each other, though — and he decided that Frank Logan's arrival in town was very fortuitous for him, indeed.

He knew that Logan was a vicious man. He'd had him checked out. Still, he was somewhat surprised at the man's reaction to the last question he'd asked.

"Logan," he asked, "how much would you charge to go after that wolf yourself?"

"More than you'll ever have, Neilson," Logan said. "That's Page's business, not mine, and he's damned good at it. In fact, he may be the best damn hunter I've ever known — except for me."

"Are you afraid of a wolf?"

"You're damned right I am," Logan said, opening the door to leave, "but remember this, Neilson — there ain't a man alive I'm afraid of, no matter how much money he's got."

Neilson had understood, and it gave him a new respect for Loren Page. He also knew, however, that no matter how many animals the wolfer had killed, it was quite a different thing to face a man who handled a gun the way Frank Logan did.

Henry Buckman was seated in the hotel lobby, patiently awaiting the appearance of Liz Archer and/or the wolfer, Loren Page.

That is, he *appeared* to be patient. In point of fact he was not, and the source of his impatience was his "employer," Eric Neilson.

Buckman knew that Neilson liked to refer to him as his foreman, when in actuality he was more of a business manager. In fact, it was Buckman's brain that had made Neilson most of his money, and sooner or later he was going to use that brain — and Eric Neilson — to make his own fortune.

Now, however, that seemed to be in jeopardy. He was worried about Neilson's condition since he had been mauled by the wolf. The man was tense, he drank too much, and at times he seemed on the verge of losing his mind.

And now there was this Logan fellow. Frank Logan was not the kind of man Neilson should be associating with. What was worse, Neilson refused to tell Buckman what he and Logan had discussed the previous evening.

It had all been going so well, and now it seemed to be on the verge of all going wrong.

He had to do something — but what?

As they approached the entrance of the Wolf Pass Hotel, both Liz and Page could see Henry Buckman seated in the lobby, no doubt waiting for them.

"There's Buckman," she said.

"I wonder what he really does for Neilson," Page said. "He doesn't look like any foreman I've ever known."

"Maybe we'll find out."

As they entered, the little man saw them. He vacated his seat and approached them.

"Ah, Mr. Page and Miss Archer. I hope that you are both well."

"We're just fine, Buckman," Page replied.

"I'm so glad. Ah, when Miss Archer told me that she was going to the doctor — "

"Is Mr. Neilson here?" Page interrupted.

"Why yes, he's in his suite."

"Well, maybe we better talk to him, huh?"

"Of course," Buckman said, "of course. This way, please. He's quite anxious to talk to you both."

As they followed Buckman to the steps, Liz said to Page, "I'll bet."

Chapter Twenty

"I believe I deserve some sort of explanation," Eric Neilson said after he'd admitted them.

He was looking at Loren Page, as if whatever had gone wrong was entirely his fault.

"Why?" Liz asked.

Neilson switched his gaze to her, looking somewhat confused.

"I'm not speaking to you, Elizabeth," he said. "Page here is supposed to be the expert."

"And I'm his partner," Liz said, "*and* you're paying me a lot of money for this — after forcing me into it."

"Elizabeth," he said, "we can talk about that — "

"All we did was come back to town to restock," Liz went on, moving toward the door. "I don't think we owe you anything but that wolf's hide — which you'll get." She opened the door and said, "Come on, partner."

"Hold on a second, Liz," Page said, surprising her. "I think maybe Mr. Neilson is right. He does deserve some sort of explanation."

Page turned to look at her and she stopped, closed the door, but remained standing by it.

"You're damned right I do!" Neilson said.

"Well now, *Mister* Neilson," Page said, turning his attention to the man, "you really don't have any call to be so upset."

"No call — "

"Has any of your stock been hit since we left?"

Neilson paused a moment, then said, "No."

"Well now, that's because that lobo's been tracking us instead of feeding off your cattle. Seems like you'd owe us some thanks just for that."

Neilson had no answer.

"We did have an encounter with the your wolf, Neilson," Page said, "and from what I can see, a lot of what you said about him is true. Among other things, he killed my horse."

"That's unfortunate," Buckman said.

"By the way, you should know that I've bought a new one. You'll have to pay for it."

"See here — " Buckman said.

"No, that's all right, Henry," Neilson said. "I agreed ahead of time to cover all of Page's — and Elizabeth's — expenses."

"That's good," Page said. "There'll also be a doctor's fee."

"Doctor?"

"I had some . . . burns treated," Page said, moving his shoulders awkwardly.

"Burns? What happened out there?"

"Let's just say that Old Gray Hair took round one from us, Neilson," Page said, "but the fight isn't over yet."

Neilson moistened his lips. "Then you . . . saw him?"

"Oh yeah, we saw him," Page said, "and he's . . . incredible. I've never seen a wolf his size before."

"Did you —" Neilson began, looking at Liz.

"She took a shot at him," Page said.

"Did she hit him?" Neilson was holding his breath.

"We think so. There was some blood left behind but . . . we're not sure."

"Then he may be dying out there!" Neilson said excitedly.

"I don't think so." Page shook his head. "If she hit him, it was with a bullet from her handgun. That'll only make him mad — and more dangerous."

"I hope you're not hinting at renegotiating your price," Buckman said.

"No, I'm not." Page looked at Neilson. "We're going to restock and leave again in the morning, Mr. Neilson. That is, unless you intend to terminate your contract with one or both of us."

Neilson didn't answer immediately.

"I, for one, would be glad to leave town, Eric," Liz said. "I've seen the wolf. My curiosity is satisfied."

"No," Neilson said quickly, "no, I want you both to get that wolf!"

Page nodded, turned, and walked to the door. By the time he reached it Liz had it open. He let her go out first, then turned to Neilson. "We'll be in touch."

"Elizabeth —" Neilson called.

The door stopped and Liz eased by Loren to see what Neilson wanted.

"I thought we might have dinner — "

"I'm sorry, Eric," she said, "but Loren and I have a lot to discuss tonight."

"I see."

The door closed and Buckman looked at Neilson.

"Those two seem to have overcome their original aversion to working together."

Neilson looked at Buckman quickly, reached for the brandy decanter, and said, "Get me Logan."

When Buckman knocked, the big gunman opened the door wide, in spite of the fact that he had a naked whore in his bed. The woman actually got up on her knees so that Buckman could see her cowlike breasts and waved at him, laughing.

"Mr. Neilson would like to see you," Buckman said coldly.

"In a minute," Logan said, and slammed the door in the smaller man's face.

The thing that Henry Buckman disliked — maybe even hated — about Frank Logan was his arrogance, and the fact that he treated Buckman as if he were insignificant.

The first chance Henry Buckman got, he was going to show Frank Logan how wrong he was.

When Buckman returned with Frank Logan in tow — Logan had not spoken to him at all during the walk to the suite — Neilson said, "All right, Henry."

Buckman backed out of the room and closed the door. "So?"

Neilson looked at Logan and, without asking, handed him a brandy.

"They didn't get the wolf yet."

"So we wait," Logan said, sipping his drink. "Now that I'm this close, I ain't in a hurry."

Of course he wasn't in a hurry, Neilson thought. He's eating, drinking, and whoring for free.

"Does it make a difference to you?" Logan asked. "I could do it now, while he's in town —"

"No!" Neilson said. "That won't be necessary. We'll wait until they bring in that wolf. As soon as I see his carcass, Loren Page is all yours."

"Fine." Logan finished his drink, put his glass down, and started for the door, but turned before he got there.

"Who's the woman?"

"What?"

"The woman with Page," Logan said, "the one with the blond hair. Is she his woman?"

"No — she is not!" Neilson said, perhaps a bit too forcefully. "She is no one for you to be concerned about."

"Sure, sure," Logan said. "Whatever you say."

Logan started back to his room — and his whore — thinking that perhaps he had gained some insight into Neilson's receptivity to the idea of Loren Page being killed.

When Page and Liz reached the second floor, he stopped her and said, "I'm gonna take a bath."

"*You're* going to take a bath?"

"Don't make a difference now," he said, looking at her. "He knows we're after him. He'll be on his lookout. Besides," he added, leaning into her and taking a sniff, "you took one."

"I'm a woman."

"I noticed."

"The doctor said you weren't supposed to get your back wet."

"I'll take a whore's bath," he said, and she knew he meant using a cloth and water from a basin.

"Meet you for supper later?" he asked.

"Sure. Want me to buy the supplies?"

"I'll give you some of Neilson's money." He reached into his pocket.

"I've got some of Neilson's money."

"You've got more than his money," Page observed. "That man is sweeter on you than — "

"Let's not talk about that," she interrupted. "His money can't buy him everything."

"Well, I don't suppose he sees it that way himself."

"Maybe not, but I told you once before it doesn't matter to me what he thinks. Shall I meet you in the lobby for supper later?"

"Fine. You know what to buy."

"How about some coffee this time?"

"Sure."

"Bacon?"

"Like I said once before," Loren Page reminded her, "let's not push our luck."

Chapter Twenty-One

Liz went to the General Store, paid for the supplies, and told the storekeeper that she'd be by to pick them up in the morning if he'd kindly have them ready. Starry-eyed, the man told he'd be happy to comply and she shouldn't mind how early she came.

She thanked him.

She went back to her room after that, gave her weapons a thorough cleaning, then succumbed to the weariness that had rapidly overtaken her and went to sleep.

When she met Page in the Lobby, it was later than she had intended, and she began to apologize for falling asleep.

"Don't," he said, grinning. "Did some snoring myself."

With mock indignation she said, "I do not snore!"

"Well," he said, "I reckon we just might be able to find that out."

They ate in the café to avoid any confrontations with Neilson or Buckman and, unknowingly, avoided meeting up with Frank Logan.

After supper they decided not to go to the saloon, but straight to their rooms — one of their rooms.

"A might early to be turning in," Page said as they approached the hotel, "but then we didn't get all that much sleep last night, did we?"

"We also got interrupted," Liz said.

They decided on Page's room.

Facing each other naked with the lamp turned down, they felt for each other in the darkness and then came together, flesh burning flesh.

He buried his face first in her hair, then her neck, then between her breasts.

"Goddamn," he said.

"What?" she asked, laughing, running her fingers through his hair as he nibbled her breasts.

"If you ain't the sweetest-smelling thing I ever saw."

"I don't know how much of a compliment that is," she said, "considering what kind of business you're in."

He went down to his knees to run his tongue around her puckered navel.

"Don't matter what kind of business a man is in," he said against her belly, "you still smell sweeter than anything he's ever seen."

She wrapped her fingers in his hair and caught her breath as his tongue probed through the tangle of fine blond hair to find her warm, wet, and waiting.

"You even taste sweet."

She tightened her fingers in his hair so she could look down into his face.

"Listen, wolfer, it ain't my fault that we both been smelling like old wolf bait for the past few days. That's been your idea."

"Oh Lord," he said, standing up and facing her, "when Old Gray Hair gets wind of you, I'll just have to sit back and wait for him to come sniffing around and then blow his head off—then I'll have to beat off every other predator within a hundred miles."

"Mr. Page," she said, "I do believe you're trying to flatter me. Perhaps you think that if you do, I'll take you to my bed?"

"The thought had crossed my mind, Miss Archer, except that we're in my room and that's my bed."

"Well, in that case—she reached for his hand—"maybe you'd consider taking me to your bed?"

"I think maybe you'd better try your hand at flattering me first . . . and then we'll see."

She moved close to him and started at his neck, moving her lips over the hard slabs of his chest, circling his small nipples with her tongue, then moving even lower, licking his navel, his belly, nipping at his wiry black pubic hair, and then running her tongue along his penis, which, by this time, was raging. She bumped the swollen tip with her nose, made a large show of sniffing him, and then stood up, grinning to herself, wondering when the last time was he smelled so clean.

"Well," she said, "you don't smell any worse than any other wolf I've been near."

He grabbed her by the arms, lifted her off the floor, and deposited her on the bed, saying, "Well, that's flattery enough!"

"Well," she said later, "I guess it's time for us to talk."

"About what?"

"We've done everything else," Liz said, "why not talk?"

"I'm not much of a talker."

"Why not?"

He shrugged. "I guess it must be from spending so much time with animals."

"You mean, hunting animals, don't you?"

"I guess," he said, "but sometimes I talk to them while I'm hunting them. I get to know them better than I've ever known any human."

"And that's why you don't talk much?"

"I guess."

"Well, then what have you been doing for the past few minutes?"

"Talking, I guess."

"You guess right."

He looked at her in the darkness, lying there on her side with the sheet down to her waist. Her breasts were leaning to her side, one against the other, and he reached out, found her left nipple, and simply rubbed his thumb over it until it was distended, then did the same to the right one.

"Maybe you're just easy to talk to," he said after a while.

"That could be, I guess," she replied, "or maybe you're just ready to talk, after all this time of not doing it."

"Maybe."

He began to rub the smooth flesh of her breasts with his fingertips, and she closed her eyes, amazed at how gentle he had become.

"Why do you hunt?"

"I thought we went through that."

"When, then," she said, changing the question. "When did you first start hunting?"

"I guess — no, I know when it was," he said. "First animal I ever hunted and killed was a grizzly. He wasn't a very big grizzly, and he was kind of old and worn out, but then I was only fifteen."

"Did you kill him?"

"I did, after dogging his trail for two and a half weeks living off berries and roots."

"Why did you go after him?"

He shrugged, as if the reason was of little importance, and then said, "He killed my pa."

They stopped talking then and he rolled over on top of her. He had to be on the top because of his back, and she had to be careful not to rake his burns with her nails.

He moved over her and she spread her legs so that his thickness slid into her easily.

"You've become very gentle," she said into his ear.

"It's easy with a woman like you," he said, moving inside of her now, starting her on her climb.

"Liz?"

"Hmm?"

"I've never felt about a woman the way I feel about you."

Something in her stomach jumped then, and it wasn't from anything he was *doing*, but from what he was saying.

"Loren," she asked, "you're not going to tell me that you're falling in love with me, are you?"

He stopped moving and raised himself up so he could look into her face.

"You're not ready to live the life of a wolfer, are you?"

"Not hardly."

"Then it isn't very likely that I'd fall in love with you," he said, and proceeded to move in her again.

"Of course," he added, "I do kind of like you."

She gasped as her orgasm seized her and she brought her hips up to him, virtually yanking his seed from him and closing her mouth over his so that their moans were sweetly muffled.

Chapter Twenty-Two

In the morning they picked up their supplies and started out again, watched — though not openly — by several people as they left town.

From the window of his suite, overlooking the main street from the third floor, Eric Neilson watched, holding an early-morning drink in his quivering hand. He'd had a dream during the night that had woken him at four A.M., and although the drink in his hand was an early one, it was not his first.

He'd dreamed that Loren Page had broken into his room while he was in bed with Elizabeth Archer and had pulled her from his bed naked, and then sicked Old Gray Hair on him. He'd woken screaming as the wolf's hot spittle was dripping on his neck . . .

The next time he saw Page he'd better have that wolf's

hide with him, Neilson thought, or he was sure as hell going to let Logan have his way, wolf or no. . . .

From *his* window on the second floor, Frank Logan watched as the whore in his bed — a red-haired one this time, but with breasts just as large as the other — called out for him to return.

"In a minute."

"It's warm," she told him.

Now that she mentioned it, naked the way he was, it was kind of cold, and she certainly did have enough hot flesh to warm him up.

He returned to the bed in a better humor than he'd been in for some time. He was eating, drinking, and fucking higher than he ever had before, and after Page was dead there was no reason to think that it couldn't go on. He was sure that he could get Neilson to see that he might need a man like Frank Logan for other things.

He slid into the whore's burning hot box, grinned, and thought, It's going to get a lot hotter, for some of us. . . .

Henry Buckman stepped out of the hotel lobby to watch them ride out. He hadn't seen Neilson yet that morning, but he knew what he'd find — a man on the edge, a man tortured by nightmares, drinking too much — a man who now wanted, along with everything else, a woman he probably couldn't have.

He wondered how badly he wanted her — then decided that it was badly enough to throw in with a man like Frank Logan.

A man who wanted anything that bad was a man who couldn't be relied on any longer. Neilson was becoming too unpredictable. He was prime for a man like Frank

Logan, who had suddenly discovered the easy life.

As Henry Buckman saw it, he had two problems on his hands right now, and he had to figure the best way to solve both of them.

From a point outside town, high up, they were watched by a pair of eyes that were not human, but were, if anything, more intent than any human eyes.

They were watching the enemy.

Old Gray Hair stood his ground, waiting. The canny wolf knew which way his enemies would take to get back up into his territory. He was going to wait there for them, let them see *him waiting.*

He was playing a predator's game, and few knew how to play it better than he did.

Chapter Twenty-Three

They traveled most of the morning in silence. There was a bite to the air, although the sun was hot enough, sitting up high in an almost cloudless sky. She could almost believe what Loren had told her about it being as hot here in Montana Territory as it was in Texas in the summer, but she still had it in her mind to leave Montana behind her eventually, with no thought of ever returning there.

They were traversing a steep incline as it neared noon when suddenly her reverie was broken.

"By God . . ." Page said, and Liz immediately looked at him and saw him looking up.

"What?" she asked, trying to follow his line of vision.

"Look, up there," he said, "the way we have to go to get back to where we were last night."

She looked up, squinting against the morning sun, and then she saw him, bold as day.

Old Gray Hair.

"What's he doing?"

"He's just standing there."

"I know that," she said, "but why?"

"He's playing with us," Page said, still looking up at the wolf. "He's letting us see him, letting us know that he sees us."

"What does that mean?"

He looked at Liz then, smiling in a odd way. "It means that he's getting cocky."

"Loren, we are talking about a wolf — "

"Animals can get just as cocky as human's can," Page told her. "He's feeling his oats because of that night in the cabin."

Page started his horse up again, and she followed, keeping alongside him.

"I'd like to talk about that night."

"Go ahead."

"Well, I'm wondering about something. I was face-to-face with that wolf for more than — I don't know — ten, fifteen seconds. He could have killed me. For that matter, he probably could have killed you. Why didn't he? Was he frightened away by the fire?"

"No," Page said, "he wasn't frightened. He was the only one, man or beast, in that room who wasn't scared or panicked — including me."

"How's your back?"

"It's fine," he said, brushing the question aside.

She hd helped him with his bandage that morning, and she knew better. His back was red and raw, and it had hurt like hell when she applied some salve that the doctor had given him, but he hadn't let on.

Big strong hunter, she thought, looking over at the wolfer

with a sudden surge of affection. He was a man who didn't need people. Liz had always needed people, had always liked them while she was growing up, liked to be around them and talk to them, but since Liz Archer had become Angel Eyes, she had taken on an attitude similar to Loren Page's — and why not? They were both hunters, weren't they?

Only what was she hunting for now, beyond this wolf? What was ahead of her after this?

She was going to have to make a decision after this was all over, she realized. She was going to have to make up her mind what she wanted from life, because drifting from town to town waiting for some young gunman to recognize her and try her out just wasn't it, not by a wide margin.

Loren Page knew what was in his future.

In his immediate future was that wolf up there, the one that was still watching them, even though they were moving closer to him. He'd wait, the wolfer knew, until they were almost in spitting distance, and then he'd dance off and hide — though he wouldn't be hiding from fear, that was for sure. He'd be waiting for his best chance to attack his enemies.

After this hunt, Page knew, there would be other hunts. *That* was his future, and nothing would change that — not even the way he was feeling about Liz Archer. They'd never be able to make a go of it together. Their lives were too different, and they were too different from each other.

Still, there was no reason why he couldn't enjoy being with her while she was around. No reason, at all.

They continued up the steep incline and Liz could still see

the wolf, standing on a small bluff, watching them, waiting. . . .

"We're getting closer," Liz said, "and he's not moving. He's not going to stand there and wait — "

"No, he won't," Page assured her. "He's already got it set in his mind when he's gonna move."

"When?"

"Oh, just . . . about . . . now!"

As he said that Old Gray Hair stood up and vanished. That is, he ran . . . although Liz hadn't seen him run, or even move. He just suddenly . . . wasn't there anymore.

"How'd he do that?" she asked as she reined in next to Page.

Page was staring up the slope, frowning and squinting.

"Page, did you see him — "

"I didn't see him move, no," the wolfer said, still staring ahead intently, "but he's not there now."

She felt a shiver go through her that had nothing to do with the cold chill in the air, and she pulled her jacket around her. Page had not made her wear the skins this time, although he was wearing his. Now she wished she had them on.

Chapter Twenty-Four

The first night of their second excursion they camped in a clearing inside a circle of Ponderosa pines. Page allowed Liz to make some coffee, which they had with hot beans and biscuits and a rabbit they had come across earlier in the day.

The jackrabbit had been a gift. . . .

They had been riding in silence when suddenly something ran across their trail, startling both of them until they realized what it was: a white-tailed jackrabbit. To their surprise he bounded away a few yards, then suddenly stopped and turned to look at them.

''Look at dinner,'' Page said, moving the Sharps off his thighs.

''Not if you hit him with that Sharps,'' she said. ''There won't be enough left to cook.''

"Well, if you're gonna do it, you better hurry before he decides to move."

At that very moment the rabbit did just that, and in mid-hop Liz drew and fired so quickly that Page did not even see her move. The jackrabbit jerked as if he were on the end of a string, and Liz holstered her gun.

When she looked at Page with a grin on her face, though, she found him watching her strangely.

"What's wrong?"

He shook his head, as if to dispell disbelief, and said, "I just, uh — that's the first time I've seen you . . . use that thing."

"Oh," she said, realizing that suddenly their relationship had changed — perhaps subtly, but it had changed, as it always did when men realized her ability with a gun.

"We'd better pick up that rabbit," she said, and pulled Blossom's reins.

She had watched with interest as Page prepared the rabbit for cooking. He skinned it, gutted it, cut off its head and legs, found a sturdy stick, and spitted it over the flame, all with an amazing dexterity and economy of movement. He cut the skin into strips and laid them out to dry while they ate.

After they'd eaten they sat with their cups in their hands, drawing as much warmth as possible from the liquid and the fire.

"Maybe the coffee smell will lure him in," Page suggested without much conviction.

"I hope not until we're finished eating," Liz replied with forced humor. "There's only enough for us."

"I understand that Neilson has a logging operation hereabouts," Page said, and Liz got the feeling he was trying to keep her mind off the wolf and maybe his mind off the way she'd handled her gun.

Why that made a difference to men she didn't know. Maybe they felt threatened by a woman who could shoot straight and true anytime she wanted to, but she would have thought Page would be different.

Maybe he just had to get over the shock.

"So I've heard."

"The man has a lot going for him."

"He seems obsessed with this wolf, though," Liz replied. "He didn't look very well yesterday."

"Like he hasn't been sleeping."

Liz chose that moment to tell Page about Neilson's encounter with Old Gray Hair. The wolfer listened intently, as if it would give him some insight into the wolf's mind.

"That explains it then," he said when she had finished. "Neilson is seeing this wolf in his sleep."

"Nightmares?"

"I've had them. I know what he's going through. He won't be able to sleep until he knows this wolf is dead." Page paused. "Old Gray Hair is haunting him."

"That's why he's so desperate for it to be killed."

"Oh, I'm sure Gray Hair is causing ranchers around here some stock, but I'd say that was the main reason. I'll tell you something, though."

"What?"

"I wouldn't have thought Neilson had enough sand to go after the wolf by himself, but I sure as hell would have thought he had more brains."

They finished their meager dinner, cleaned the utensils, and put them away, except for the coffeepot and one tin cup.

"It's getting colder," Page said, although Liz was quite

sure that he was used to it and leaving the pot out for her benefit.

She didn't argue.

"I'll take the first watch," she offered. "I'm not very sleepy."

"All right." He untied his bedroll and, using his saddle as a pillow, settled down with the Sharps right alongside him.

Liz moved closer to the fire, poured herself some coffee, and swore to herself that it was the darkest night she'd ever seen.

It was past time for Liz to wake Page, but for some reason she did not.

She would, because she knew she needed sleep if she was to be alert the next day, but she just didn't feel like it just yet. The cold, coupled with the fact that Old Gray Hair was out there somewhere — probably *watching* her — did wonders for her alertness.

Remembering what Page had said about staring into the fire, she made a special effort to preserve her night vision and, at one point, she could have sworn that there were two glowing eyes out there staring intently at her — with malice!

"Time," Page said, sitting up.

"I know," she said, startled. "I would have woken you in a few minutes."

Page got to his feet and squatted near the fire. She noticed that his Sharps moved as if it were a part of his body. Also, he was again wearing the Navy Colt.

"I'll bet you'd swear you'd seen glowing eyes looking into camp from the darkness."

"How did you know?"

"Everything you're going through now I've been through," he said. "You don't want to sleep, you can *feel* him watching you — "

"All right, all right," she said, pulling her own bedroll over, "I'll go to sleep."

"You'll need it, believe me."

"You're the expert," she said, with more confidence than she really felt.

Positive she'd never be able to close her eyes, she lay down. The next thing she knew, Page was shaking her awake for a breakfast of coffee and biscuits.

Chapter Twenty-Five

"Should we talk about it?" she asked.

It was past noon of the second day, and they hadn't seen Old Gray Hair yet, just his sign. That wasn't what was on Page's mind, though. Liz decided to get it out in the open and deal with it.

To Page's credit, he didn't pretend not to know what she was talking about.

"I hadn't heard anything about you until Neilson told me," Page said, "and that was just talk — until I saw you outdraw a jackrabbit in mid-flight."

"So?"

He shrugged and said, "You just surprised me, that's all."

"You sure that's all?"

"What do you mean?"

"Why can't a woman handle a gun as good or better

than a man without people looking at her funny?''

He paused a moment, as if to think, and then said, ''I don't know. I guess there are just some things men think are just for men.''

''Like what? Hunting, *bounty* hunting — ''

''Just things,'' he said, ''and maybe we're wrong.''

''Maybe.''

They rode a while in silence, as had become their pattern. They'd ride quiet for a while, then talk some, then fall quiet again.

Abruptly, Page pulled to a stop as they were approaching the sight of the cabin fire.

''What's wrong?''

''The tracks are too fresh.''

''That means it's not a false trail, doesn't it?''

''You fish?''

''What?''

He looked at her then and asked, ''Have you ever fished?''

''No. My pa used to, but he never took me. Why?''

''He's got us hooked good, Liz'' — Page studied the ground — ''and he's reeling us in.''

''What's that mean?''

''He's been leading us around by the nose ever since we started out, and now all of a sudden he's stopped. *Now*,'' he said, ''I think he's ready to let us find him.''

''So what's going to happen?''

He shook his head slowly. ''I don't know. All I know is that we're playing his game, and maybe we should change it.''

''How do we do that?''

''It depends,'' the wolfer said, ''on how patient this particular wolf is.''

"This is your game, Loren. You call the hand."

"All right. All right. We go this way," he said, pointing east, "and not to the cabin site."

"But if he's up there — "

"If he's up there," Page interrupted, "then he's waiting for us — and he'll wait a long time before I'll ride where he wants me to."

Liz frowned at Page and wondered just how the wolfer saw this hunt — and all his hunts? As a contest? As a battle of wits between man and animal?

Whatever the case she had no choice but to follow his lead, because without him she'd be easy pickings for Old Gray Hair. She was more accustomed to facing men, who were predictable.

This animal surely wasn't — and neither was Loren Page.

They traveled due west, toward Idaho Territory, and Page explained.

"When he sees that we're not following, he'll follow us."

"You hope."

"No, he'll follow," Page said, with assurance, "especially if he's carrying your bullet. He'll want us bad, then, bad enough to follow and wait for his chance."

"How long will that take?"

"Like I said, depends on how patient he is . . . and I have a feeling this one is real patient."

Old Gray Hair was becoming impatient.

He still carried the pain in his haunch and was eager to taste the blood of his enemies, but they were no longer following him.

He waited a while near the place where he'd been injured, but when they didn't come he stood up and padded back down the slope until he found the place where they had veered off.

Now he was the hunter, following sign, trying to catch up, and when he did he would wait no longer.

He would take his revenge and be done with it and then get back to his feeding.

Chapter Twenty-Six

They kept riding west, deeper into the forest with the Rockies looming above them, and eventually they came to Eric Neilson's logging operation. There were cabins for the loggers, a mess hall, equipment, and, further on by the lake, flumes to carry the logs down the slope once they were cut down. The bulk of the equipment they saw was unrecognizable to either of them, because neither knew anything about the logging business.

They were four days out of Wolf Pass up to this point, and Gray Hair had been on their trail almost two.

"That's a patient wolf," Liz said as they looked down at the logging operation.

"Yep."

"And you're a patient man."

"Yep."

"And we're out of food."

They'd eaten the last of the dried rabbit, and all they'd had that day were some berries and roots.

"We can go down by the lake and fish," Page said, "or we can ride into camp there and see if they'll feed us."

"Which do you say?"

"Well, if we go down to the lake, Old Gray Hair's eyes will probably pop out of his head, because we'll be out in the open."

"And if we ride into camp?"

He looked at her. "That sure would frustrate that old wolf."

The camp was bustling with activity as they rode in. They stopped one man and asked who was in charge.

"That'd be Zeke Graves," the man replied.

"Where can we find him?"

"Over in the office." The man pointed to a smaller cabin among a group of larger ones that were used as bunkhouses.

"Thanks," Page said, but the man wasn't looking at him, he was looking at Liz.

"Thank you," she said, smiling.

"You're welcome, ma'am."

They rode over to the office, dismounted and secured their horses, then knocked on the door.

"Come in!" a voice called gruffly from inside.

They entered and saw a large man with an overstuffed belly, wearing suspenders and chewing on a huge, unlit cigar. He was leaning over a desk that was covered with papers and what looked like a blueprint. He was talking to another man who looked up as they walked in and couldn't take his eyes off Liz.

The big man, who must have been Graves, looked up then and spotted them.

"Mr. Graves?" Page asked.

The man stood up straight, walked around the desk, removed the cigar from his mouth, and peered intently at them.

"You're the wolfer," he said suddenly, pointing at Page with the dry end of the cigar. "The one working for Mr. Neilson, right?"

"That's right."

"You're gonna kill that devil wolf."

"I'm gonna try."

"Yeah, that lobo," Graves said, popping the cigar back into his mouth, "he's cost me a few men, you know."

"Killed them?" Liz asked.

He looked at her approvingly and then said, "Killed a few, run off a few. Scared to stay and work."

"I see."

"What can I do for you people?"

"We thought we might get a meal from you," Page said, "maybe some extra supplies, coffee, maybe some jerky —"

"You can have as much as I can spare if it will help you get that wolf."

"We don't need much," Page said. "Wouldn't want to weigh ourselves down."

"This your partner?" Graves asked, indicating Liz.

"That's right," Page said.

"Not bad work if you can get it, huh?"

"Not bad."

"Dave," Graves said to the other man, "take them over to the mess and fix them up with a hot meal. Then get together whatever supplies they need."

"Sure, Zeke."

"Thank you," Page said to the foreman — or whatever

you called the head of a logging operation — but Graves had gone back around his desk and was examining his blueprint again. He simply waved his hand without looking at them, and they followed Dave outside.

"I sure don't envy you your job," Dave said to Page. The man was in his late twenties, not tall but broad and powerful, probably just the right build for a logger. He didn't seem to realize that Liz was also hunting the wolf. She put that down to a man once again putting her in what he thought was her place.

"What about yours?" she asked.

"Mine?" he asked, looking at her. "Nothing exciting or dangerous about mine."

"Do you climb these trees?"

"Sure."

"All the way to the tops?"

"Sometimes."

"And that's not dangerous?"

"Naw," he said, puffing his chest out, showing off for the pretty lady, now, "not when you know what you're doing."

"I know what I'm doing when I hunt a wolf," Loren Page told the man, "and it's still dangerous as hell."

"I suppose. . ."

"Then again," Page said, "that tree that you're climbing isn't waiting to rip your heart out, is it?"

While they were in the mess eating, Dave went out to arrange for their supplies and for their horses to be fed.

"God, this is good," Liz said as she dipped a piece of fresh bread into the stew they were eating. It was filled with chunks of meat and vegetables swimming in a thick, brown gravy.

"They sure eat well on a logging operation," Page remarked.

"Maybe too well," Liz said. "I'm not sure I want to go out there again."

Page looked at her and she realized that he might be taking her seriously.

"Oh, I'm going, don't worry," she said.

"I think I'll ask Graves if he can put us up for the night."

"Why?"

"So we can be well rested come morning," he said, looking at her, "and go out and get that wolf."

Graves agreed, but not without reservations.

"We can find you a bunk with the men," he told Page, "but we're not used to having a woman in camp."

"Will that be a problem?" Liz asked.

"Shouldn't be. We can set up a pallet for you here in my office, and I'll make sure the men stay away from the door. Okay?"

She grinned. "Okay."

Graves stared at her and then took the cigar out of his mouth. "Of course, I've got the only key, but I think I can be trusted." He was looking at Page, his eyes twinkling.

She patted Graves on his ample belly and said, "I'm sure you can."

Chapter Twenty-Seven

In the morning, after a fitful night's sleep, Liz came out of the office and went over to the mess. As she entered, looking for Page, she saw Graves — and she drew the attention of all of the men.

Graves stood up, barked something at the men that she didn't catch, and then approached her. "How did you sleep, Miss Archer?"

"Not very well."

"Ah, a good breakfast'll fix that up," he assured her. "You mind eating with the men?"

"No, not at all. Have you seen Page?"

"I'll get you a place over here." He led her to a table. "Most of the men are finished, anyway. What'll it be? Flapjacks? Eggs, bacon, some biscuits? We got it all."

"Mr. Graves," she said, suddenly wondering why the man was babbling so. "Where is Page?"

Graves looked at her kind of sheepishly and then said, "I was supposed to keep you busy until he got a good head start. I guess maybe I — "

"That bastard!" she snapped, and some of the men's heads turned toward her. "He planned this. That's why he wanted to stay the night."

"I guess you might be right about that, miss," Graves said. "All I know is he got up early this morning and said he was going after that wolf, and that I was to keep you busy."

"Well, you tried," she said, and turning, she walked out of the building.

He came up behind her and grabbed her arm.

"Hey, miss, that forest ain't no place for you to be riding around alone, not with that wolf out there."

"Mr. Graves, I'm getting paid to kill that wolf, just like Page is. You wouldn't want me to just sit and not earn my money, would you? Not when we both have the same employer."

"No, I guess I wouldn't."

"Would you have my horse brought out, please?"

"Sure, I'll have Dave bring her out. You wait right here."

"Don't stall me — "

Graves put both his hands up shoulder high and said, "I give up. I can't stall any longer."

"All right."

"While Dave gets your horse, I'll get you some supplies."

"Just some coffee, jerky, and a pot, if you can spare it," she said. The jerky was for when she got hungry and the coffee to keep her warm.

And when she found Loren Page, she was going to make it plenty warm for him too.

Old Gray Hair was closing in on his prey, moving easily despite the slight limp the bullet in his haunch was causing. He didn't feel the pain anymore, though, because he was concentrating on his enemies.

Soon it would all be over.

Chapter Twenty-Eight

Liz called on everything she had learned from Page during the past week to pick up his trail, and since the trail was fresh — barely an hour old — she was finally able to.

She also picked up something else, though, something that Page had showed her enough times for her to recognize, and something that made her breath catch in her throat. She halted Blossom and dismounted so that she could study the ground the way she had seen the wolfer do, just to be sure.

And she *was* sure.

There were other tracks, *behind* those made by Page — Old Gray Hair's.

The wolf was hunting the hunter.

She had thought that she'd catch up to him fairly quickly, but as darkness began to fall she knew she was mistaken.

Both of them, man and wolf, were moving at a good pace, and it was all she could do not to fall behind. A couple of times she thought she might have lost the trail, but she had observed Page long enough to be able to pick it up again.

As she rode throughout the day she cursed Loren Page thoroughly in her mind, again and again. What the hell did he think he was doing, protecting her? Was it because of the remark she'd made while they were eating yesterday? Or was there another motive?

Did he want this wolf all to himself?

She didn't pretend to know the real reason why Loren enjoyed hunting wolves and other dangerous animals, but was there something involved here, something like . . . possessiveness. Sure, he'd been against having her as a partner all along — hell, so had she — but she'd thought they'd worked that out.

Maybe she'd been wrong.

As it got darker, it got colder, and she pulled her jacket closed in front, pulled the collar up, and jerked down on her hat. She knew she ought to make camp, but if Page was making camp himself, she'd rather catch up and stay with him.

If for no other reason, she could tell him that the wolf was on his trail — if he didn't already know that.

God damn the man, was that what he was doing out here? Offering himself up as bait, waiting for the wolf to make a move on him?

Hadn't he said that the wolf would want revenge on the one who had injured him, and wasn't that her?

She reined Blossom in abruptly and listened intently. It was quiet, much too quiet.

Had the wolf doubled back? Was he now behind her, stalking her?

Blossom pawed the ground nervously, tossing her head, and that's when Liz knew that something was amiss.

"Easy, girl," she said, patting the bay's neck. "You smell that nasty old wolf, or do you just smell that nasty old bastard of a wolfer?"

She kept stroking the bay's neck, trying to keep her calm and quiet while peering into the darkness, trying to see between the trees. The moon was out, but the peaks of these damn trees were screening much of its light, and she suddenly realized that it had gotten pitch black out.

And suddenly, just like that, she *knew* that Old Gray Hair was out there, looking at her, and that it wasn't just her imagination.

Loren Page wasn't the bait.

She was.

Secreted in the darkness, with his wolfskins pulled closely around him and his Sharps close at hand, Loren Page watched and waited. He wondered if Liz would realize that she was being used as bait, that he had known that she would follow him and had, indeed, counted on it.

Oh, he knew that the wolf was on his trail, but he also knew that when the wolf got wind of Liz — the human who had injured him — she would become his primary target.

Page had used his skills as a hunter and tracker — moving quietly, never losing sight of his prey while staying out of sight himself — to parallel Liz for most of the day, after he had left false trail for her to follow. Old Gray Hair had tailed him while he had been laying down the false trail, and had followed him back until they both became aware of Liz's presence in the forest. At that point, Gray Hair had begun to stalk Liz, and Page had begun to parallel her progress, keeping a sharp eye out for the wolf.

He hated to do it this way, but the simple fact of the matter was this: that wolf was going to wait as long as he had to before making a move for her, waiting for the moment when she would be separated from Page. What Page knew he had to do was engineer the split so that he could watch over her and make sure she was safe.

Now he sat astride his horse — an animal who had become used to the wolf smell because his rider smelled like one — and watched and waited for the wolf to go after Liz.

He only wished it wasn't so damned dark.

Liz had figured it out, and she was even madder than she had been before, when she thought that Page had left her behind to *protect* her.

That son of a bitch!

Blossom continued to paw the ground nervously, and it occurred to Liz that, in her fear, the horse could possibly throw her and leave her at the mercy of the wolf. The logical move — to her untrained mind — was to dismount to avoid that.

Loren Page watched Liz intently and in his mind he was telling her, whatever you do, don't dismount!

Liz dismounted and moved around in front of Blossom to caress the horse's nose and calm her down. Her Winchester was still in the scabbard on her saddle.

Page cursed.

She was on her feet and the rifle was out of her reach!

He dismounted — even though he knew he shouldn't — and began to wend his way through the trees.

He had to get closer.

Most of the moonlight was blocked by the trees, but with his excellent night vision he was able to see . . . fairly well.

He's out there, Liz thought.

They're both out there — the son of a bitch and the wolf.

Suddenly, Blossom screamed and pulled her head out of Liz's grasp. The frightened animal lunged, knocking Liz over, and ran into the forest.

Idly, as she lay on the ground stunned, she thought, This wouldn't have happened if I'd stayed mounted.

That was when she saw the wolf.

Old Gray Hair could smell the small human, and he could almost taste her warm blood. He watched her intently, circling, ever circling, until he found the position that he wanted — and went for his revenge.

Chapter Twenty-Nine

He was standing there in a shaft of moonlight, as if he had planned it. His eyes were on her steadily and his mouth was open. In fascination she watched his breath escape in great cloudy gusts, and his saliva drip to the ground.

Slowly, she leaned on her left hip so she could get to her gun. As she slid it out of her holster, she took her eyes off the wolf—*for only a second!*—and when she looked back he was gone.

Now she got up on one knee with the gun held ready and tried to see into the darkness, wishing she had her Winchester. He could have been standing there just out of her sight, watching her, or he could have been circling her, waiting for a chance to dart in and tear her apart.

All she could do was wait.

Page saw the wolf in the moonlight, but when he lifted the

Sharps the animal was suddenly gone. The wolfer tried to move closer without making noise. He leaned against a tree, holding the Sharps at shoulder level, waiting for him to appear again.

''Come on, you son of a bitch,'' Liz said under her breath — talking to the wolf, not to Loren Page.

The wolf was her first priority — she'd take care of the wolfer later.

When it happened it happened too quickly, and Page realized that he'd been outfoxed.

The wolf came in suddenly, but he had been circling Liz, and when he made his move, she was between the wolfer and the wolf.

Old Gray Hair had known where Page was all along!

She almost didn't see him and then there he was, a streak of silver and gray, moving faster than she would have thought him capable.

Angel Eyes brought her gun up and pulled the trigger, kept pulling until it was empty. Only her superior reflexes enabled her to get off all 5 shots before the wolf could cover the ground between them.

And it kept coming.

She remembered what Page had told her about not stopping the wolf with a .34 — and he had been right, damn it!

Frantically, Loren Page maneuvered for position, trying to get to a point where Liz wasn't in the way and he could get a clear shot with the Sharps. He heard her fire 5 times, and the beast kept coming.

That damned .34!

Now the wolf seemed to be moving in slow motion, and she could see his muscles bunch as he got ready to jump on her.

She wanted to close her eyes — but she couldn't.

Page fired!

Liz heard the shot, like a clap of thunder, and as the huge wolf was in mid-leap, so close to her that she could feel his hot breath, he was suddenly jerked away as if by a giant hand.

Page came walking out of the darkness as Liz was getting to her feet. From force of habit she was ejecting the empties from her gun and shoving in fresh shells. When Page reached her, she was standing over Old Gray Hair, gun ready in case the beast should jump up.

"He's not going to get up," Page told her, coming alongside. "Not after a shot from the Sharps."

He prodded the carcass with his foot, and the animal didn't move. It was lying on its left side, and there was a bloody hole on its right side — along with six other, smaller holes, one fired a few nights ago by the cabin, and the others fired only moments earlier.

"Look at him," Page said, squatting down. He ran his hand over the dead animal from one end to the other. "He's the size of a small grizzly."

"You were out there all along," she said.

He stood up, looked at her, and said, "We got him, Liz. We got him."

"Son of a bitch," she said, and swung her right fist.

Chapter Thirty

They rode into Wolf Pass with the carcass of the wolf tied behind Loren Page's horse.

"Why don't you go over to the hotel and get cleaned up," Page told Liz. "I'll find Neilson and deliver the wolf."

"I'll stick with you," she said, and it was the first words she'd spoken to him since punching him in the mouth. He still had the swollen lip from the blow, which had actually knocked him down.

He'd gotten up and apologized, tried to explain, but she wasn't having any. After that he'd just retrieved his horse, tied the carcass to it, and they headed back.

"All right," he said, "have it your way."

"For a change?"

"Liz —"

"Let's find Neilson and get paid," she said, "then we can officially end this partnership."

They rode up to the hotel, dismounted, and while Page stayed outside with the carcass, Liz went inside to look for Neilson.

She walked up to the desk and asked the clerk, "Is Mr. Neilson in his suite?"

"Yes, he is," the clerk said, but a voice from behind Liz said, "He's been saiting for you there since you left."

She turned and saw Henry Buckman, dapper and unctuous as ever, standing behind her.

"Shall I see you up?"

"Sure."

As they were ascending the steps to the third floor, he asked, "Did you get it?"

"We got it."

"Fine," Buckman said, and led the rest of the way in silence.

At the door to the suite Buckman stopped and said, "I . . . think there's something your friend Mr. Page ought to be aware of."

"Then tell him," Liz said. "I'm not interested."

Buckman frowned and wondered what had happened out in the forest to provoke such a response.

"I really can't . . . talk to him, you know," he said. "I'd rather tell you. It's quite important."

"So's getting my money for that wolf," she said, and knocked on the door.

Buckman sighed, produced a key, but before he could insert it the door opened and Neilson stood there, swaying unsteadily with a half-filled glass of brandy in his hand.

"Elizabeth?" He narrowed his eyes, trying to focus on her through an alcoholic haze. He stood there, looking at her expectantly, and then asked, "Did you get him? Did you get the devil?"

She nodded. "Yes, Eric. We got him."

"Where is he?" he asked excitedly.

"Go and look out your window."

Neilson turned and staggered to the window, pulled aside the curtain, and looked out.

"Jesus," she heard him whisper. "Jesus . . ."

He turned from the window and staggered back toward the door. For a moment Liz didn't know what he was going to do, but then she realized that he intended to go downstairs to take a close look at the wolf — his nightmare laid to rest.

He brushed past both her and Buckman and hurried down the hall. Liz started after him but Buckman put a hand on her arm. She pulled it away and glared at him.

"You don't like me, Miss Archer."

"You're right about that, Mr. Buckman," she said, "but don't be offended. Today I don't like anybody."

"I really must talk to you about your friend — "

"I don't have any of those today either. Excuse me."

When Liz reached the street, she was shocked by what she saw. Eric Neilson was standing next to Loren Page's horse, laughing and running his hands through the dead wolf's thick hair. After a moment, he actually put his *face* against the wolf's carcass, laughing hysterically.

She turned to see Buckman come out of the hotel with a look of distaste on his face, walk over to Neilson, and begin talking to him earnestly, in a low voice. He finally put his hands on Neilson's elbows and began to lead the larger man away from the wolf.

Page stepped in front of them. "I'd like my money, Mr. Neilson."

"Later." Buckman looked at Page and then at Liz. "Later, when he's calmed down. Come by the suite at nine this evening, and you'll be paid."

Page and Liz exchanged glances, and then she said, "All right."

As was his custom Frank Logan walked naked to the window of his room and looked out. He did this almost every hour — just in case somebody he should know about was riding into town. Not necessarily Loren Page, but *anyone*.

This time, as he looked down at the street, he saw two horses tied in front of the hotel, one of them with a huge wolf tied across its back.

"Damn," he said, staring at the wolf. He had to hand it to Page. It took nerve to go after a beast like that — on the animal's own terms.

"What's wrong, sweetie?" the whore asked from the bed.

This one was a blonde, not quite as buxom as the other two but just as expert — which meant that what she lacked in . . . meat . . . she made up for with talent.

"Just something you don't see every day, honey," he said, letting the curtain drop back in front of the window.

He turned back to her and she sat up, letting the sheet fall away. She had the smallest nipples he'd ever seen on a woman, which actually made her breasts look bigger. They were small — the nipples, that is — until he thumbed them, or sucked them, and then they suddenly blossomed. He had found himself fascinated by the transformation.

She wasn't real pretty, however, which is why he made her spend a lot of time with her face between his legs.

He walked up to her, his penis standing straight up, and decided that if she remarked on how small it was he was going to slap her.

As he reached the bed he said, ''Suck me.''

She opened her mouth and complied, with considerable expertise.

He was waiting for a knock at the door, and this was just as good a way to wait as any.

Chapter Thirty-One

Liz was in the bathtub — and this time she was taking a long, hot soak — when there was a knock at her door.

"Go away."

"Miss Archer," Henry Buckman's voice called, "I really must talk to you about something very important."

"Go . . . away!"

"Miss Archer — "

"In one minute I'm going to fire a shot through that door!"

There was a pause, and then Buckman's voice said, "As you wish — but we *will* talk!"

"Sure, sure . . ." she said, waving her hand in the air, spattering water around.

She was mad at all men today, and Loren Page in particular. All she wanted to do was get her money from Neilson — if he was capable of counting that high any longer —

and then leave this town and Montana behind her.

She was drying herself off when there was another knock at the door.

"Who is it?"

"It's Loren Page, Liz."

"Go away."

"Liz, we have to talk."

Everyone wanted to — no, *had* to — talk to her today. What was it that made her so popular?

"No!"

"Liz — "

Angrily she snatched up her gun and almost squeezed one off through the door — high, of course — when she remembered something Tate Gilmore had told her. Never draw unless you plan to kill a man, and if you plan to do it — do it!

Tate Gilmore — probably the only man she'd open her door to right now.

"Go away, Loren," she said, pushing the gun back into the holster. "I'll see you in Neilson's suite — for the last time."

She waited to see if he would try anything else but then heard his footsteps as he walked away.

She dried off, dressed, and went downstairs for dinner. After dinner, she'd go to the suite and collect her blood money. When she had it, she'd go to San Francisco. She'd never been there, and with five thousand dollars she'd be able to see it the way it should be seen.

Frank Logan was in Neilson's suite with a brandy in his hand, watching the rancher carefully.

"They're coming up here to get their money tonight?" he asked.

"That's right."

"I don't like that, Neilson. Change the plans."

"I can't. Buckman told them to be here."

"If I were you, *Mister* Neilson" — Logan fixed him with a hard stare — "I wouldn't be here."

Neilson frowned. "Where would you be?"

Logan thought it over. "At your ranch. They'll come out there for their money, and I'll be waiting."

"For Page."

"Of course."

"You're not to touch the woman."

"Of course not." Logan walked toward the door. "The woman is all yours — "

"That's right."

" — and Page is all mine."

Liz was leaving her room to go to dinner when she saw a man come down from the third floor. He was a tall man, clad in black, wearing twin pearl-handled Colts. He paused to look at her with a grim set to his mouth, then turned and walked down the hall and into a room.

She thought she knew him, but she couldn't be sure.

She was eating dinner when Loren Page entered the dining room. He had bathed and was wearing fresh clothing for a change.

He wanted to be forgiven — bad.

He walked to her table and sat down.

"We're gonna talk," he said, "and the only way you're gonna avoid it is to have me thrown out."

"That's not the only way," she said confidently, "but go ahead."

"Liz, my job was to get that wolf, and it wasn't going to happen while we were together."

"Is that your explanation?"

"Damn it," he said loudly, then realized he was attracting attention and lowered his voice, "we got him, didn't we?"

"Sure, and now we'll get paid and then say good-bye."

"But how will we say good-bye? That's the question."

"Well, I guess we'll just have to wait for the answer, won't we?"

He stared at her, then sighed in frustration and left.

As he walked out, Henry Buckman walked in and Liz groaned.

"Excuse me, Miss Archer." Buckman stopped at her table. "May I sit, please?"

"Why not? Everyone seems to be."

"Your friend, Mr. Page, is in danger."

"Again?" She stared at him. "All right, Mr. Buckman, what kind of danger?"

"He is in danger of being killed."

"By who?"

"Frank Logan."

That was it! The man with the pearl-handled Colts! Tate Gilmore had mentioned him, and once or twice over the past year she'd heard his name.

"Logan's a bounty hunter," she said. "There's no price on Page's head."

"Apparently the grudge is personal."

"Why are you telling me this?"

"Because Logan has persuaded Mr. Neilson that it would be better if Mr. Page were dead than to pay him all that money."

"Wait a minute. Neilson is paying Logan to kill Page so

he won't have to pay Page for killing the wolf?''

''That's essentially correct,'' Buckman said, ''although it was not Mr. Neilson who proposed the bargain.''

''And what about me?''

''You? Mr. Neilson will give you anything you want. He desires you almost as much as he did the death of that wolf.''

''So then he'll pay me.''

''Yes.''

''And then try and get me to stay?''

''Yes.''

''Well, he won't succeed.''

Buckman shrugged. ''That is between you and him.''

''You don't care, do you?''

''It does not matter to me who he sleeps with.''

''What does matter to you, Henry?'' Liz asked. ''What's your angle in all this?''

''I live quite well off what Mr. Neilson pays me,'' Buckman said, ''and I would prefer to continue to do so.''

Liz thought a moment, then felt she had a handle on Buckman.

''You're afraid that Logan will go after you next.''

''You are astute, and it is entirely possible.''

''So warn Page when he's in the suite to collect.''

''I'm afraid Mr. Neilson will not be in the suite to pay off.''

''Wait a minute.'' She put her fork down with a bang. ''You said he intended to pay *me*!''

''He will be at the ranch. You may come by tomorrow and collect.''

''And Page? What if he comes too?''

Buckman stood up. ''You will collect your money, but he will collect something else entirely.''

She stared at Buckman. "Lead."

"Well put, Miss Archer," Buckman said, "very well put. I leave this matter in your hands now."

"Thanks."

She tried to finish her dinner but could not. Her appetite had been ruined.

What should she do? Warn Page? Hadn't he risked her life to get the wolf?

She owed him something, and she went upstairs now to pay him off.

Chapter Thirty-Two

"I don't know why you didn't want to ride out here last night and shake the money out of the bastard," Loren Page said as they rode up to the Neilson ranchhouse.

Both of them had checked out of the hotel and were ready to leave Wolf Pass and Montana Territory directly from Neilson's ranch.

"We had other things to do last night, didn't we, Loren?" she said.

Yes, they had other things to do. She'd done the only thing she knew to keep him from riding out to Neilson's house last night.

She'd slept with him.

And she'd enjoyed it, because the sex between them was good — and because she knew that today he'd be paid back for what he'd done to her, for the danger he'd exposed her to.

As they approached the house the front door opened and

Eric Neilson stepped out. Quite a transformation had taken place since the last time they'd seen him. He looked like the self-assured, successful businessman he'd been when she first met him.

He didn't look like a man who had thrown in his lot with a killer.

"Good morning," he greeted them.

"What was the idea of running out last night, Neilson?" Page demanded. "You owe us money."

"I pay my debts, Mr. Page," Neilson said, "just as you should pay yours."

"What are you talking about?"

Instead of answering, Neilson looked at Liz. "Come inside, Elizabeth."

"What for?"

"Your money."

"I'll take it out here, Eric."

"We need to talk."

"No, we don't."

Neilson fixed Page with a malevolent stare. "Are you going with him?"

"Eric, I want my money and then I'm leaving Wolf Pass — alone — and I won't be back. Is that plain enough for you?"

"It's plain enough," he said, with a pained look on his face.

He turned on his heel, went inside, and returned moments later with a bulky brown envelope. He tossed it out to her, and Liz caught it by pure reflex. She guessed that she was hardly Eric Neilson's favorite person at the moment.

"Hey," Page said, getting Neilson's attention. "Where's my payoff?"

Neilson grinned tightly and said, "Your payoff, wolfer, is behind you."

Page frowned and then turned, as did Liz, and looked behind him.

"Hello, Page," Frank Logan said. He was standing with his arms folded across his chest, the pearl handles of his Colts gleaming as if they had just been cleaned.

Liz was watching Loren Page and swore that she saw something that very closely resembled fear pass over his face.

"Logan," she heard him say beneath his breath.

He looked at Liz then, still frowning, and said, "You knew. That's why last night — "

"Payoff," Liz said, "and payback."

"Because of the wolf?" he asked, disbelief written all over his face.

"Get off your horse, Page, and move away from the lady," Frank Logan said.

Page gave Liz one last look, then dismounted, holding his rifle.

"Put the rifle down."

Page obeyed and Liz sidestepped Blossom out of the line of fire and then dismounted.

"You're not going to shoot him in cold blood, are you, Logan?" she asked. "I'd heard that wasn't your style."

"You heard right, lady," Logan said. "You've got a handgun, Page. I know it."

"I've got one."

"Get it."

"No."

"What?"

"I can't match you with a gun, Logan," Page said. "I

know that. If you want me dead, you're just gonna have to go ahead and do it.''

"Loren — " Liz started.

"That's fine with me, Page," Logan said. "I've been waiting a long time for this, ever since that big cat killed my brother."

"I couldn't help that, Frank — "

"Sure you could," Logan said, "if you wanted to. You and Danny were partners. You hunted together, you trusted each other. Danny trusted *you* and you let that cat kill him.''

"I tried — " Page said, haltingly. "Danny was too close. I *told* him to move, Frank — "

"Forget it, Page." Logan moved his hands down to his sides by his Colts. "It's over. This is the end. Either you strap on a gun now, or I'll shoot you down like . . . like an animal.''

"Start shooting, Frank."

Liz felt it had gone far enough and spoke up.

"Hold it, Logan."

Logan frowned at her. "What do you want, lady?''

Liz walked over until she was standing within five feet of Page.

"I'm not going to let you shoot an unarmed man, Logan.''

Looking annoyed, Logan said, "Get out of the way."

Liz stepped to her right, and now she was standing in front of Page.

"Liz, don't — " Page said.

"Shut up, Loren," she said. "I'm saving your life."

"Not at the cost of your own."

"Hardly," she said. "I'm still mad at you."

"Liz — "

"Loren," she hissed, "let me do what I do."

"You hiding behind a woman, Page?"

"I can't match you with a gun, Frank" — Page shrugged helplessly — "but maybe she can."

"You're crazy," Logan said. "You're both crazy. I'll just kill her and then you. What's the point in that?"

"He's not a damn jackrabbit, you know," Page said.

"Get out of the way, Page," she replied.

Page walked over and joined his horse on the sidelines. Buckman was watching from inside the house, and Neilson was still on the porch.

"Logan, this is not our deal!" he shouted.

"Our deal is off, Neilson!" Logan replied. "You'd better get off that porch."

Neilson backed up quickly until he was inside the door.

"Lady, you're making a big mistake," Logan said.

"Maybe," she said.

Her gun was on her right hip so when her left hand moved Logan didn't overreact. She reached inside her collar and removed the bandanna, allowing it to unfurl.

She saw Logan react then, his eyes narrowing, and then widening.

"I know that — "

"You ready, Logan?"

"Angel Eyes," he said, and went for his gun.

Of the four men watching — Neilson, Buckman, Page, and Logan — Logan was the most surprised, Page the least, because he had seen her catch that rabbit in midair.

Still, this is no rabbit, he thought. This is a known gunman — that is, *was*.

Buckman and Neilson were quite surprised — though not as much as Logan was when her bullet struck him in the chest before either of his hands could even touch those shiny pearl handles.

"It wasn't very nice of you not to tell me about Logan," Page said as they rode away, leaving Neilson and Buckman with the problem of disposing of Logan's body.

"Why, were you scared?"

"Terrified."

"Good. You deserved it for what you did to me."

"I guess I did. Are you still mad?"

"Yes."

"Mind if I ride along with you a ways?"

"Until the border, I guess."

"Which border?"

"I don't know. Which one were you heading for?"

"I don't know either."

They rode on in silence for a while and then Page said, "Odd that Neilson should have had that much money on hand since he had no intentions of paying me."

"He *is* a wealthy man."

"Yes, I suppose he is."

After a few moments Liz gave him a sidelong look and asked, "Why? How much did he pay you?"

"Enough," he said, and then giving her a sidelong look asked, "how much did he pay you?"

"Oh . . . enough," she said, "I guess."

And they rode on, each wondering how much *enough* was.

On Sale Now!

THE GUNSMITH
430
Show Girl

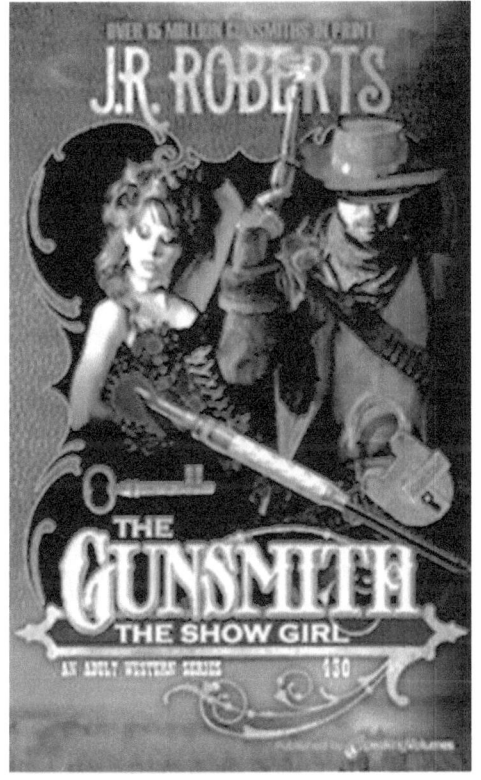

For more information
visit: www.speakingvolumes.us

On Sale Now!

THE GUNSMITH
431
The Science of Death

For more information
visit: www.speakingvolumes.us

On Sale Now!

THE GUNSMITH
432
The Bank Job

For more information
visit: www.speakingvolumes.us

On Sale Now!

THE GUNSMITH
433
Little Amsterdam

For more information
visit: www.speakingvolumes.us

On Sale Now!

Lady Gunsmith
A New Adult Western Series
Books 1-4

Roxanne Louise Doyle is Lady Gunsmith,
a hot, sexy woman who is unmatched with a gun…

For more information
visit: www.speakingvolumes.us

On Sale Now!

MOUNTAIN JACK PIKE *series*
by
Award-Winning Author
Robert J. Randisi (J.R. Roberts)

For more information
visit: www.speakingvolumes.us